D0363335

The Beast and the Bethany

Revenge of the Beast

For Liza Meggitt, or 'mother dearest' as you insist I call you.

Vengeance shall be mine.

J. M. P.

For Jack

I. F.

First published in Great Britain 2021 by Farshore
An imprint of HarperCollins*Publishers*
1 London Bridge Street, London SE1 9GF

farshore.co.uk

HarperCollins*Publishers*
1st Floor, Watermarque Building, Ringsend Road
Dublin 4, Ireland

ISBN 978 1 4052 9891 9
Printed and Bound in the UK using 100% Renewable Electricity at CPI Group (UK) Ltd
1

A CIP catalogue record for this title is available from the British Library.

The Beast and the Bethany

Revenge of the Beast

Jack Meggitt-Phillips

Illustrated by Isabelle Follath

The Beastly Beginning

When Ebenezer Tweezer was eleven years old, the world was much younger.

Instead of cars on the streets, there were horses and carriages. In place of phones and computers, people would communicate via letters and hopeful shouting.

There was no such thing as photographs, and so if you were the sort of person who liked to capture the moment whenever you happened to be wearing a nice outfit or eating a pretty meal, you would have to travel around with your own personal portrait artist. Electricity was nothing more than a silly word back then, which meant that you could only read books past bedtime if you had an extensive collection of candles.

In short, it was a pretty rotten time to be alive. And for poor Ebenezer, it was especially rotten, because he was a deeply unpopular child.

It's hard to say exactly what made him so unpopular. Perhaps it was because he had a smug-looking face, or it might have had something to do with the fact that his outfits were always rather extravagant – filled with ruffles and colourful patterns.

Whatever the reason, it was clear that the other children did not care for young Ebenezer. He was never invited to their feasts, jester jousts, or theatre trips, but this didn't deter him from arriving uninvited. In fact, Ebenezer would spend most afternoons lurking outside *The Muddlington Pie Shoppe,* because he knew that, from time to time, the children would gather there and challenge each other to impromptu pasty-eating competitions.

More often than not, though, Ebenezer would spend entire days outside the pie shop, and no children would arrive. Ebenezer would use the time to practise his conversation skills by talking to the wall. He'd say things like;

"Isn't it a fine day we're having?"

Or:

"Have you seen that new comedy by Willy Whatshisname?

No, I didn't get any of the jokes either."

And:

"Such a rotter about that plague, isn't it?"

Invariably, the wall didn't have anything to say. But Ebenezer didn't mind, because he saw all of these one-sided chats as terribly good warm-ups for the real thing. He was sure that if he could only strike upon the right topic of conversation, or wear the right number of ruffles on his shirt, then the other children would let him join in with their pasty-filled merriment.

On one such day, when he was lurking outside the pie shop, Ebenezer became aware of a commotion taking place in the square. The town crier had given up his usual shouting about the wonderful deals available at his wife's haberdashery and was now crying something in an urgent voice. Ebenezer wasn't able to hear the exact words, because the commotion and uproar in the street was too loud.

Serious-looking men, wearing some very silly scarlet capes and green stockings, were dismounting from their horses. They each carried a trumpet in their hand, as if it were a weapon, and their faces were grave with worry.

"You there, boy!" shouted one of them. Ebenezer saw there was a crest on his cape, which read *Division of*

Removing Rapscallions in Secret. "Have you seen the deadliest creature that has ever tormented this earth?"

Ebenezer was pretty sure that he would have remembered such a creature, but he was a well-behaved child, and he wanted to be as helpful as possible. It took him about twelve seconds to flick through his memories.

"No, I'm almost certain I haven't," said Ebenezer. "Is this a game of hide-and-seek? No one's agreed to play it with me yet, but I don't think you're meant to ask for help."

"This is no game, boy! If we don't capture the creature,

before it regains its strength, there's no telling what might happen," said the cape-wearer.

"Oh, deary me," said Ebenezer. "I wish I could help. But like I said, no creatures have crossed my path. Sorry."

The cape-wearer seemed to take this remark as a personal insult. He huffily returned to his horse and trotted away from Ebenezer. The rest of the cape-and-stocking-wearers continued their search – bursting into establishments, and asking pointed questions – but Ebenezer's attention was soon drawn elsewhere, when he spotted three children approaching the pie shop.

"I hear they caught it in Lady Morgana's basement. Apparently she'd been keeping it hidden from the Division for centuries," said Nicholas Nickle, an unpleasant boy, with a suitably unpleasant face.

"No one lives for centuries, so that's clearly not true, brother dearest," said Nicholas's distinctly un-dear sister, Nicola Nickle. "*I* heard that the creature used to be the size of a small hill, until the Division fed it a trumpet. One of Morgana's neighbours said they saw the creature deflating like a balloon and whooshing out of the house."

"I WANT SOME STOCKINGS!" said Nicco Nickle, the youngest child of the ghastly family.

The Nickles were generally viewed by the rest of the neighbourhood as menaces, but Ebenezer was not in a position to be fussy about friends. As they approached, Ebenezer tousled the ruffles on his shirt, and tried to remember his small-talk training.

"Isn't it a rotter about this willy comedy, eh? No, I didn't get the plague at all," said Ebenezer. A frown wrinkled his brow. "Hang on a moment, I think I might have got that a bit up-jumbled."

The Nickles' faces lit up. Ebenezer mistook this as an expression of friendship, so his face lit up too.

"Well, well, well – look who's here for another beating. It's only Mr Ebenoozer Loooooseerrrr," said Nicholas.

"I love it when you call me that," said Ebenezer, deadly serious. "I read somewhere that it's very important for friends to have nicknames for one another."

"We're not your friends, Ebenooozer. I thought we showed you last time what happens when you call us that," said Nicholas.

"Hmm? Oh yes, that game where you chase me whilst throwing sticks and stones is great fun," said Ebenezer. "But perhaps this time we could just have a little chat instead? The wall and I have been practising for hours."

However, it soon became clear that the Nickles were not in the mood for a spot of sparkling conversation. The three of them charged at Ebenezer, chasing him through the square and out onto the fields that led to the back of his house. They hurled names, insults, and the occasional rock at the back of his head.

Ebenezer was comfortably able to outrun them, because he was blessed with a pair of long, gangly legs. As he ran, he tried to convince himself that this was just another game, even though he knew, deep down, that it wasn't. Like everyone else, the Nickles had taken an immediate dislike to Ebenezer, and he was powerless to do anything about it. There was no amount of shirt-shopping or wall-talking that was going to make them like or respect him.

But then, as he was sprinting through the final stretch, he stepped on something squishy. He looked under his shoe, and found that the squishy something was a worm-sized blob of grey. As he peered even closer, he was able to make out three black eyes, two black tongues, and a dribbling mouth. It had a set of tiny limbs, and its breath stank of boiled cabbage.

"Help me," said the squishy something, as he scraped it off his shoe.

Ebenezer was so shocked by the voice that he dropped the squishy something. He quickly picked it back up, and dusted away the specks of mud from its eyes.

"Terribly sorry about that," he said. As he looked at the squishy something, he knew he was holding something extraordinary. For a few seconds, he just stood gazing at it, but then, he remembered his manners. "My name's Ebenoo – I mean, Ebenezer."

"And I am a beast. Please, you're my only hope – help me."

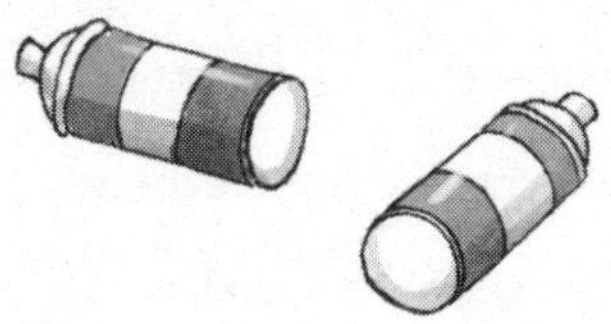

The De-Beasting

"What a creature – so unlike anything I've ever seen! Such beauty, such poise, such grace – you deserve the world, and I'm going to jolly well make sure I give it to you."

Five hundred years later, Ebenezer was soaking in his morning bubble bath, whispering sweet nothings to the reflection in his handheld mirror. Over the centuries, he had learned that mirrors are much easier to talk to than walls – especially when you have a rigorous potion and skincare routine that gives you a face as beautiful as a twilight moon.

"Why the sad face?" Ebenezer asked himself. "The morning bath has always been a happy occasion!"

Over the course of his long, long lifetime, Ebenezer had soaked in almost 186,275 baths, and they had all been

very happy occasions indeed. Today, however, there was something amuck.

For one thing, Ebenezer's wind-up rubber ducky was missing. This was a serious blow to proceedings, because Raphael was a ducky who had performed tricks and sang moving sea shanties every morning since the beast had vomited him out.

For another, there was something dashed peculiar about the smell in the room. Thanks to the beast, Ebenezer was accustomed to baths that were bubbled and salted with only the very finest products a man can bathe in, and yet there was a distinctly cheap and nasty odour leaking out of the bubbles – as if someone had replaced his salts with dishwasher powder.

For the third, final and most-disturbing-of-all thing, there was a smudgy, greasy-fingered message from Bethany on his handheld mirror:

OI, GITFACE. NO TIME FOR BATHING TODAY. DE-BEASTING TO BE DONE.

Naturally, Ebenezer had ignored the message, because it was his long-held belief that there is always time for a bath. He believed that you often need to take a bath right at the moment when other people would have you believe that there is no time for one.

However, the message continued to vex and irk, because it made him wonder what Bethany had planned for their day, and eventually his curiosity could take it no more. He cut his bath short by a couple of hours, threw on some loungewear, slippers and a dressing gown, and made his way downstairs.

His journey was fraught with confusion and peril, because certain items in the fifteen-storey house seemed to have gone walkabout. Confusion clouded his face when he noticed that all the furnishings from the velvet suite had been replaced with deck chairs and whoopee cushions. The confusion gave way to alarm when he found that his favourite collection of beautiful paintings had been taken off the wall. In their place was a selection of doodles and unconvincingly proportioned stickmen, which had been graffitied on to the wallpaper and signed by Bethany.

"No, no, no!" said Ebenezer, sprinting downstairs to address Bethany in his best 'I'm really rather cross with you' sort of voice. "What on earth are you doing?"

"Stupid question," said Bethany. She was quite right, because it was perfectly obvious that she was trying to

remove a piano from the front room of the house. "Gimme a hand, gitface. We've gotta get this on to the street with the other stuff."

"I shall do no such thing!" said Ebenezer. "I'm not going to help you rob me."

"We're not robbing you, we're helping you. Claudette and I have been working our flipping butts off," said Bethany.

And then, as if to show off her butt-working, Claudette the Wintlorian purple-breasted parrot flew into the house. Her feathery forehead was slightly damp with sweat.

"That's the last of the dancing teapots done, poppets!" she said, spreading her wings in a 'Ta-da!' pose. "Hi-de-hi, Ebenezer! Has Bethany told you about our wonderful de-beasting mission?"

"De-beasting?" asked Ebenezer.

"Yeah," said Bethany, matter-of-factly. "De-beasting."

Claudette sank her talons into the piano, and assisted Bethany in her efforts to drag it out of the room. They were neither strong enough nor strategic enough to move the instrument, without causing great damage to the walls and floors.

"Why do we need to de-beast?" he asked. "Claudette *killed* the beast, I'd say that's a pretty thorough de-beasting already."

"How very dare you, I'm not a killer! I just happened to accidentally eat it, and I've been feeling simply awful ever since," said Claudette, puffing her feathery belly.

"Don't feel awful. The beast was a wicked, terrible monster who tried to eat me!" said Bethany.

"Oh yes, I know that, but you've somewhat misunderstood me. I really have been *feeling* awful. Indigestion, or something like that. I haven't had a good night's sleep in weeks," said Claudette.

"Still not seeing what any of this has to do with you two pinching all my things," said Ebenezer.

"It's not *all* your things, it's just the stuff the beast vomited out for you. Claudette said it would be good for us," said Bethany. "I don't want to look at all the stuff, and neither should you. Like this piano – do you remember who you fed the beast to get it?"

Ebenezer looked at his slippers, with a shameful expression upon his face. In order to get the piano, he had fed the beast Patrick – another Wintlorian purple-breasted parrot, who happened to be a cousin of Claudette's. Claudette had been remarkably forgiving about the whole thing.

"All right, we can sell the piano and maybe some of the gold-plated cutlery," said Ebenezer. He reluctantly joined in with the piano-moving operation, as they squeezed it through the front door. "But we mustn't go too crazy with it."

Once they got outside, Ebenezer realised they had already gone far too crazy. The lawn was covered with various gifts that the beast had vomited out for him over the past five centuries – all the things Ebenezer had asked for at the beginning, which he thought might help him make friends, and all the other stuff in the centuries that followed, which he got just for himself, or to make other people jealous.

Ebenezer's bath salts were there, and so was Raphael – the wind-up rubber ducky. There were pudding fridges, a self-decorating Christmas tree, a mind-reading vacuum cleaner that tidies rooms whenever you think they look a bit dusty, televisions the size of bed sheets, an astronaut suit – and many other strange and wonderful things. Ebenezer felt as if his whole life with the beast was on display for the world to see.

"Bethany, are you trying to kill me or something?" he asked.

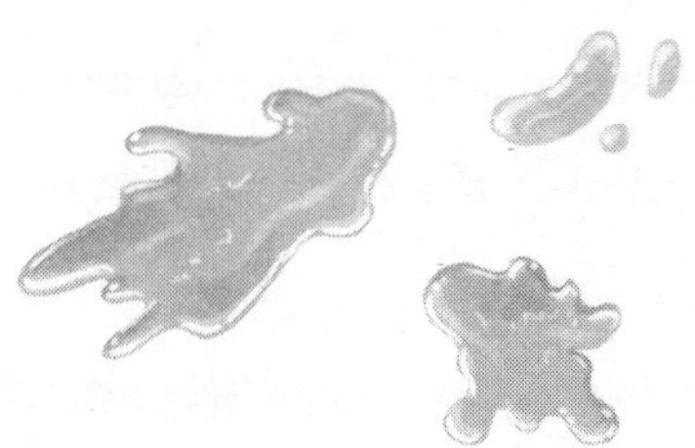

The Great Game

"I'm dying," said the beast, all those centuries ago.

Ebenezer looked behind him. The Nickles weren't far away, and they were each armed with sticks, rocks and mud. He looked back at the beast, and wondered what to do.

"If I don't have something to eat soon, I'll disappear entirely. Please, show me some kindness."

Ebenezer had never been needed by anyone before. He generally felt like he got in people's way – especially his mother's. It was a rare sensation to feel like he could actually help someone, and he seized upon the opportunity by feeding the beast a few handfuls of grass and daisies.

"Very kind of you," said the beast, in a soft and slithery voice. *"But that's the wrong kind of kindness. None of this will give me the strength I need."*

Ebenezer looked behind him again, and saw that the Nickles were almost within rock-throwing distance. He darted over and picked some blackberries from a nearby bush.

"Well done for trying," said the beast, through tiny, gritted fangs. "But this isn't exactly a proper meal now, is it? Surely, somewhere, you can find me something with . . . a pulse?"

Ebenezer quickly searched around, but the only living thing he could find was a spider, who was dozing on a cobweb between two bushes. He apologised to the spider, before offering it to the beast.

The beast devoured the spider and its home in one bite. A dribbly smile spread across its lips, and its small body grew ever so slightly larger.

"Keep up the good work and bring me MORE!" said the beast.

Fortunately for Ebenezer, a butterfly happened to fly right into his path. Unfortunately for the butterfly, Ebenezer fed it to the beast.

The dribbly smile stretched wider, and the beast's body expanded a little more.

"Clever little boy – now you're getting the hang of it,"

said the beast. "*We'll soon get me back to full strength.*"

Ebenezer was pleased to have made the peculiar creature happy, but his pleasure was interrupted by a rock, which sailed through the air, whacked his shoulder, and ripped his ruffled shirt.

Nicholas had thrown it, and he had a pointed stick in his other hand. His siblings were both carrying splodgy mud balls.

"There's no running away now, Ebenoozer Loooser," said Nicholas. "I'm awfully dangerous with sticks like these."

Ebenezer instinctively covered the beast with his other hand, so that the Nickles couldn't hurt it. He smiled weakly at the three of them.

"Congratulations, you win!" said Ebenezer, trying to speak in a light, chummy tone. "Such a smashing game. Is it my turn to chase you now?"

"This isn't a game, you friendless Looozer," said Nicola. She threw a mudball, which hit him right in the stomach and left a horrid mark on his shirt.

"Please, don't be like that. You might like me, if you gave me a chance," said Ebenezer. "And I'd really appreciate it if you could be careful. This shirt is made from the finest silk."

This did little to improve Ebenezer's relationship with

the children. Nicco threw his mud ball and left a nasty bruise on Ebenezer's kneecap.

"Owww. This is my third most favourite pair of trousers," said Ebenezer, rubbing his kneecap with the hand that was being used to cover the beast.

"What's that?" asked Nicholas, pointing with his pointy stick.

Ebenezer saw that the beast was wiggling angrily in his hand. *"How dare you treat my servant like this! Don't you know who I am?"* it asked Nicholas.

"Is that a pet worm? You really are such a loooser, Ebenoozer," said Nicholas.

"Right, that's it!" The beast closed its three black eyes and shut its dribbling mouth. It started to wiggle its blob of a body, and made a low humming noise as it moved from

side to side. Then, all of a sudden, its eyes opened again. The beast spread its mouth wide open and vomited out a blaze of fire.

The Nickles screamed and ducked to avoid the flames. They dropped their remaining weapons, and turned a palish, papery colour.

"Oh my goodness, I'm so terribly sorr—" began Ebenezer, but then he saw how the Nickles were looking at him. There was fear in their eyes, and that fear looked awfully like respect.

"*Throw me at the one with the unpleasant face, if you want to have some fun,*" whispered the beast, in its slithery voice.

Ebenezer had never been on the throwing side of the game before, and he fancied giving it a go. He threw the

beast at Nicholas. As it sailed through the air, the beast hummed and wiggled again, before vomiting out a cloud of itching powder.

"Graahoowwe!" said Nicholas. He followed this up by adding "Ooofy!" and "Eeekyarrrgh!", as he scratched his body.

Ebenezer laughed. As he laughed, Nicola and Nicco ran as fast as their legs could carry them, but the beast wasn't finished with Nicholas yet.

The beast perched on Nicholas's shoulder at this point, turned around to face Ebenezer. Its three eyes were hungry for revenge. "*Watch as I melt this child into a puddle. It's my way of saying thank you.*"

"Oh good gosh no. That's very kind, but there's really no need. I don't want anyone to be puddled on my account," said Ebenezer.

But part of him wondered what a puddled version of Nicholas might look like. He walked over slowly, and, for the first time in his life, he felt what it was like to have power over someone else. It was surprisingly enjoyable to see the terror in his previous tormenter's eyes.

"Please, let me go," begged Nicholas.

"No, no, no – that's not how this game works," said

Ebenezer. "You never listen to me when I ask you to stop throwing things. This is part of the fun isn't it?"

Nicholas begged for his life in sobs and wails. Ebenezer saw the beast laughing at this, so he laughed as well.

"Please, I'll do anything," blubbed Nicholas. "Get that thing off me!"

"*Anything*?" said Ebenezer. He thought for a moment about what he might be able to claim as his winner's prize. "Well, if you really mean it – then I'd like you to be my friend. Oh, and could you get the other children to invite me to their feasts and jousts?"

Nicholas nodded, and his bottom lip wibbled with terror.

"*And if you or your snotty little friends tell anyone about me, then I will hunt you down,*" said the beast.

Nicholas nodded and wibbled so vigorously that it looked like his head might fall off. Ebenezer smiled, but not with weakness this time. He scooped the beast off his shoulder and said, "You may leave now . . . *Nicholooser.*"

Nicholas didn't laugh at this little joke, as he ran to join his siblings, but this didn't matter, because the beast was laughing and looking at Ebenezer with pride. It even seemed to have grown a little stronger.

Ebenezer continued the walk back to his house, carrying

the beast in his hand. Every now and then, he would interrupt the journey to pick up things for the beast to eat; worms, insects, and anything else he thought it might like. By the time they reached the back door, the beast was the size of a tennis ball.

"No one's ever done anything like that for me before," said Ebenezer. "My mother usually just says that my life will improve once I stop being annoying."

"*Your mother's a fool. Would you like me to melt her into a puddle?*" asked the beast.

"No, absolutely not! And please stop threatening to puddle people," said Ebenezer. He looked down sadly at his shirt, which was ripped and dirtied with mud. "But if you have anything that can fix my outfit, I would be very grateful."

"*Why fix something broken, when you can have something new and shiny instead?*" said the beast, with a dribbly grin. It wiggled and hummed and vomited out a gold-buttoned shirt made from the finest materials.

"This is the prettiest vomit I've ever seen," said Ebenezer, as he stroked the shirt's soft fabric. "You'll stay with me, won't you? I think you and I could make an excellent team."

"*Yes, I think you and I are going to be great friends,*"

said the beast, making Ebenezer blush. "*And don't worry, I promise that you will never, ever get rid of me.*"

PINK GOBLIN

The Yard Sale

Bethany had set up a stand on the street next to the lawn, with a sign that read:

WE'RE GETTING RID OF EVERYTHING BEASTLY – ALL PROFITS WILL GO TO THE ORPHANAGE

"We need to take that down – right away," said Ebenezer.

"Oh, don't be like that, old sport. Bethany and I spent all morning making it," said Claudette.

"I don't care," said Ebenezer. "The beast was always clear that I should keep it hidden from the rest of the world. It said that if people knew about its powers, then we would

attract unwanted attention from the *Division of Removing Rapscallions in Secret* and other people."

"The beast isn't here any more, and I like the sign. So it's staying up," said Bethany. She folded her arms to indicate that this was the end of the conversation.

Ebenezer was about to ignore the arm-crossing and plead once more, but their conversation was interrupted by the arrival of their first customer. Eduardo Barnacle was a pompous boy with nostrils the size of fists, and he was usually the first person to show up to any street fair or gathering.

"Ah, Mr Tweezer, how thrilling to find you here. I wasn't going to come, because I feared this might be another one of Bethany's pranks," said Eduardo.

"Bog off, Barnacle!" said Bethany.

Eduardo did nothing of the sort. He picked up 'The Golden Boy' (Ebenezer's favourite painting) and took a deep sniff.

"Mmmnh! You can really smell the artistry in this one."

"It's not for sale. None of the paintings are," said Ebenezer. Claudette gave him a pointed look, but he didn't change his mind.

Other people might have shopped elsewhere, in the face of such rudeness, but Eduardo Barnacle was not your usual sort of customer. He strolled around the lawn, browsing for something else that might be suitable to purchase. His nostrils led him to a cheeseless cheeseboard – a diamond-encrusted one that the beast had vomited out after Ebenezer brought it a small family of beavers to eat.

"What about this fine culinary specimen? Is this one for sale?" asked Eduardo.

Ebenezer hadn't used the diamond cheeseboard for over fifty years, but he didn't want to part with it. He was just about to tell Eduardo to take his nostrils elsewhere when he was treated to a furious kick from Bethany – and it was the sort of kick that told him he shouldn't push his luck any further.

"Humph, fine then," said Ebenezer to Eduardo. "But make sure you look after it."

"Don't you worry, Mr Tweezer, I shall treat it as if it were part of my very own soul." Eduardo took out his fat wallet. "How much do I owe you?"

Ebenezer and Bethany looked at each other. Neither of them was good with money; Bethany because she had never really had any, and Ebenezer because he had always had too much. Claudette was also pretty useless, as she was accustomed to using Wintlorian yen.

"Three thousand and two pounds," said Ebenezer.

"A bowl of fruit and a brand-new pencil case," said Bethany, at the same time.

Ebenezer, Bethany and Claudette excused themselves from Eduardo for a moment. After a heated conversation they settled upon the price of £12.73.

It was an excellent deal, and Eduardo was so delighted that he also took away Raphael, the wind-up rubber ducky. Eduardo spread the word that the yard sale wasn't an elaborate Bethany prank, so soon nearly everyone in the neighbourhood turned up to get a little something for themselves.

Miss Muddle – an eccentric and experimental sweet-maker – picked up the pudding fridges in exchange for some curly-whirly fizzle sticks, whilst the lizard-looking lady, who worked at the zoo, bought a scooter for the chimpanzees at the wonderful price of £3.87. Even Jared Kettlefletch, who owned *The Late-Night Pranking Emporium*, came along, and he usually hated mingling with the rest of the neighbourhood.

"What are you doing here?" asked Bethany.

"Same as anyone else," said Jared Kettlefletch, grinning a gold-toothed grin. "I've come to see if there's anything shiny I might be able to take home. What about you,

Bethany? It's been so long since you've visited my shop. You should see some of the new booby traps I've got in store. They're proper horrid."

"Nah," said Bethany. "I'm done with all that. No more nasty pranks."

Jared Kettlefletch went home with the sharpest knife from the set of gold-plated cutlery, and the rest of the items sold within the space of an hour. The piano and the mind-reading vacuum cleaner being the last to go – these were sold to the bird-keeper for twenty worms.

"How 'bout eighteen and a half?" asked the bird-keeper. He was a large, pleasant man, but he was careful with money.

"It's twenty or nothing, tighty-pants," said Bethany. "And if you argue any more we'll sell it to someone else."

"All right, but this better include delivery. I ain't gonna be expected to drag it all the way to my shop, am I?" asked the bird-keeper.

Bethany agreed to include delivery in the price, and slipped the worms into her pockets. Ebenezer looked around the lawn – there was nothing left, save for the paintings that he had refused to let go.

"I feel like you've just given my life away," said Ebenezer.

"Only the beastly bits. You should let us sell the paintings too," said Claudette.

"Never, I bought these myself! If we got rid of them we wouldn't be de-beasting, we'd be de-Ebenezering!"

Ebenezer would never have been able to purchase the paintings without the beast, but Claudette didn't say anything, because he was already clearly upset. Bethany collected the box of money and the other more peculiar profits, whilst Ebenezer picked up the sign and stand. They headed back towards the house, but Claudette stayed behind.

"Afraid I'm going to have to tootle-off, poppets," she said. "Lots of songs to prepare for tonight's rehearsal."

Claudette was a little slow at taking off – probably something to do with the sleepless nights, they thought – and when she left, Ebenezer took a final, sad look at the empty lawn. His life felt incomplete without all the things that the beast had vomited out.

"Don't worry, you're gonna feel *sooo* much better – I promise," said Bethany.

They went into the house, where Ebenezer was unsurprised to find that he didn't feel sooo much better. He felt distinctly worse each time he saw a space where one of the beast's things used to be.

Ebenezer went up to his room and put on his favourite pair of trousers to cheer himself up. As he was deciding which shirt to wear, he came across the gold-buttoned one, which the beast had vomited out for him all those centuries ago.

It was a magical shirt, which had grown and shrunk as Ebenezer changed shape over the years. The fine materials were still as dizzily dazzling as it had been when the beast had first vomited it out.

"Oi, gitface, are you coming back down here or what?"

shouted Bethany, from downstairs. "We need to drive this stuff over to the orphanage."

Ebenezer knew he should probably tell Bethany about the shirt, and the other items in his wardrobe that she had missed out as part of her great de-beasting mission, but he didn't want to lose it, or see it worn by somebody else.

"If you're not down here in ten seconds, I'm gonna pour milk into all your shoes!" shouted Bethany.

With a slight twinge of guilt, Ebenezer slipped the shirt over his body. It tightened around his skin for an uncomfortable moment, but then the fabric relaxed and he could breathe easily again. It was strange, impossible even, but it felt like the shirt was breathing with him.

"I'll meet you in the car now!" Ebenezer shouted down, stroking the shirt's silky cuffs. "And I think you're really going to like my outfit . . ."

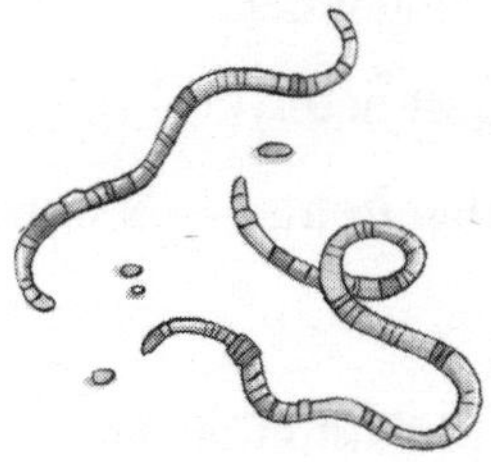

The Day of Do-Gooding

The fabric of the gold-buttoned shirt was as smooth and silky as a perfectly prepared chocolate mousse, and it felt just as exquisite on Ebenezer's skin, as it had done all those centuries ago.

He'd last worn it on the most recent New Year's Eve, when the beast, in a rare generous mood, had vomited out a personal firework show for the two of them. Ebenezer giggled as he thought about the Bottle Rockets and Roman Candles, fizzing around the beast's attic.

"See. I told you the de-beasting would make you feel awesome," said Bethany.

Ebenezer's giggle was brought to an abrupt end. An awkward cough took its place.

"I wasn't smiling about that," he said, returning his attention to the steering wheel.

"What was it then?" asked Bethany.

"Just some joke about a hippopotamus," said Ebenezer. "It doesn't matter."

He took the turning into the orphanage, and as usual Bethany got all weird and fidgety. She always did this, because she felt rotten returning to where she had spent the unhappiest years of her life. And yet, she also felt a thrill of nervous excitement whenever they visited, because this was the place where she saw Geoffrey – a previous victim of her pranks, who had now become something of a friend.

"I shouldn't be carrying these worms," said Bethany. She removed them from her pockets, as Ebenezer parked up. "If Geoffrey sees me with them, he'll think I'm trying to shove them up his nostrils. You give them to the orphanage."

"I shall do no such thing. The worms are your problem."

"I'm not gonna be seen dead with them. Either take them in your hands, or take them up your nostrils. Your choice," said Bethany. Ebenezer reluctantly opted for the hand option, whilst Bethany

collected the box of money and the other things they had received at the yard sale.

Once outside, their eyes were assaulted by the full majesty of the orphanage's ugliness. It looked like the kind of building that had completely given up on trying to impress people – an architectural equivalent of someone who freely picks their nose in public. Usually, the place was noisy with children, but on this occasion it was suspiciously quiet.

"Where's Geoff—?" began Bethany, before correcting herself. "I mean, where's everyone?"

As if in answer to her question, the new director of the orphanage shuffled out of the building to greet them. His name was Timothy Skittle, and he didn't seem fond of unexpected visitors.

"Oh no," said Timothy, to Ebenezer. "Please don't tell me you're here to drop off another child. I can barely keep control of the ones I've got."

"We're here to bring money and presents to help the orphanage," said Bethany.

Timothy ignored her contribution to the conversation.

"Don't leave her with me, I'm terrible with children," he pleaded.

"There's nothing to worry about. Bethany's staying

with me. I picked her up from here about a month ago," said Ebenezer.

"You're not the Bethany, are you?" asked Timothy, who now seemed even more worried.

"Yeah, that's me," said Bethany, thoroughly pleased with herself. "I bet you've heard some pretty awesome things."

"I've heard some pretty *awful* things. About how you put wasabi in tubes of toothpaste, and hid fake spiders in the cornflakes. The other children are terrified of you," said Timothy.

"Terrified? But they were jokes!" said Bethany. "Did Geoff— Did *all* the children sound scared of me?"

"I've barely had time to meet them all, let alone ask for their opinions on you. But from everything I've heard, you're one heck of a beastly brat," said Timothy, cowering in terror.

'Beastly' was an unfortunate choice of word. Bethany was already hurt to hear that her reputation was swinging so low, but this tipped her over the edge.

"I am NOT a beast. I am trying to be a better person. Look at these worms we've brought you!" she said, pointing at the wriggling minxes in Ebenezer's palms.

"Oh great, some worms and another child are all I need," wailed Timothy. "Although I can't see how you could be any worse than Gloria."

Bethany did not recognise the name 'Gloria', which was odd because she knew pretty much all the children at the orphanage. She had spent time and energy devising personalised pranks for each and every one of them.

"Gloria?" asked Bethany.

"Yes. Gloria Cussock," moaned Timothy. "She's the daughter of Mr and Mrs Cussock – the ones who run the theatre. She arrived the same day that I did, and she's been making my life a misery ever since."

"What happened to the Cussocks? I had no idea they'd died," said Ebenezer, though he wasn't surprised. When you get to 512, people constantly perish around you.

"Nothing's happened to them, they're brimming with good health," said Timothy. "They just can't stand their daughter. I keep trying to send Gloria back to them, but they won't open the door."

"Where is this Gloria? Can I meet her?" asked Bethany.

"You can't and you shouldn't," said Timothy. "Gloria ordered the other children to carry her around the neighbourhood on her portable throne, because she wanted to buy herself some snacks and outfits for some sort of rehearsal show they're going to tonight. It features a talking penguin, or a yodelling pigeon – something stupid like that. Gloria's making me go as well."

"It's a singing parrot, and it'll be an awesome evening," said Bethany. "If you don't want to go, why don't you just tell Gloria to bog off?"

Timothy let out a shrieky laugh. "Nobody tells Gloria to bog off. Once she's made up her mind to do something, or make somebody else do something, there's no stopping her," he said.

Bethany thought Timothy was a weakling. She would have liked to give him some pranking tips to help bring Gloria into line, but she worried that it wouldn't have been a 'de-beasting' sort of activity.

Instead, she and Ebenezer handed over the profits from their yard sale. Timothy wasn't very grateful. "Mustn't let

Gloria find out about the money," he mumbled to himself, as he walked back to his office. "She'd make me use it to get her another pair of tap shoes."

Bethany had expected the meeting to go rather differently. She had hoped for a parade of gratitude in honour of her thoughtfulness, but instead she had been called beastly. She angrily jammed the seat belt into the clicker when they got back to the car.

"Thank goodness that's over," said Ebenezer.

"Nothing's over. Nothing's even close to being over," said Bethany. "You heard Timothy and those people at the sale – everyone thinks I'm a monster. We need to take our de-beasting to the next level."

"Please, no more de-beasting," groaned Ebenezer.

"Tough. We need to make up for all the bad we've done," said Bethany. She bit her lip, before speaking in a grave voice. "We need to do some do-gooding."

"Anything but that, please, Bethany – have some mercy. I tried doing do-gooding before, centuries ago, and it just ends up with people throwing sticks and mud at you."

But Bethany was committed to the course at hand. After dropping off the piano and the mind-reading vacuum cleaner at the bird-keeper's, she made Ebenezer pull over so that they could put some proper thought into the matter.

"What do you want to do first?" asked Ebenezer, with little enthusiasm.

"I dunno. How should I know what good people do?" asked Bethany, right back at him.

Both of them had a rummage around their heads to see if they could come up with any ideas. They were severely inexperienced in the art of do-gooding.

"I think we're going to have to find a good person and copy what they do," said Ebenezer.

They drove around the neighbourhood to see if they could spot any good people. After about twenty minutes, they felt like it might have been easier if they'd gone dodo-spotting instead.

"What about that one over there?" asked Bethany, as they drove past the comic shop.

"No one with eyebrows that twirly could possibly be a good person," said Ebenezer. "How about that one?"

"Nah, she looks like the sort of person who would give an apple as a trick-or-treating present," said Bethany.

As they drove around, they ruled out several other members of the neighbourhood. They were both getting crabby about how difficult it was to find someone suitable, but then they almost knocked down a kindly old lady who seemed like a perfect fit.

"I've never seen someone with a pleasanter face," said Ebenezer. "And look, she's apologising to us even though we nearly ran her over."

"Yeah, she's ace. Definitely the sort of person who would give you a big whack of chocolate if she found you trick-or-treating," agreed Bethany.

Ebenezer tootled the horn, whilst Bethany wound down the window to speak with her.

"Excuse me, kindly old lady, but we were wondering if we could ask you a question or two?" asked Ebenezer. The lady was delighted to be called kind (but not quite so thrilled to be called old) so she nodded and leaned her ear nearer to the car. "First of all, would you say that you're a kind and good person?"

"Oh, I'm not sure about that," said the kindly old lady. "I'm sure there are lots of people out there who are much kinder and nicer than I am."

"That's exactly what a good person would say. Well done, you've passed the test!" said Bethany. The kindly old lady was delighted, even though she had no idea that she was being tested. "Now, my friend Ebenezer and I wanna be good. What things can we do to be like you?"

The kindly old lady didn't know how to answer this question. She looked to the sky as she wondered what would be the most useful thing to say. Soon Bethany grew impatient.

"Tell us about today, what are you planning to do right now?" she asked.

"Well . . . first, I'm going to drop off a bag of washing at the laundrette, and then I'm going to go for a spot of late lunch. I'm thinking maybe a soup or something," said the kindly old lady. "Sorry, that probably isn't much help to—"

"That's ace. Just what we needed!" said Bethany.

She wound up the window, and Ebenezer stepped on the accelerator. When they got back to the house, they threw all their dirty clothes into the washing machine, and prepared a cream of nutmeg soup.

"Do you feel any different?" asked Ebenezer.

"Nah. We must have done something wrong," said Bethany.

They washed the clothes again, this time on a 'super-duper spin cycle' setting, and prepared themselves a cream of parsnip and mushroom soup. They still didn't feel so much as a twinge of do-goodery. They did, however, feel rather ridiculous.

"We're being a bit stupid, aren't we?" said Ebenezer, chuckling.

"Yeah. Total flipping idiots," said Bethany, contributing a few chuckles of her own. "That lady must have told us the wrong tasks – the nitwit. Let's go back and see if we can find her."

"Do you think we have enough time?" asked Ebenezer.

They looked at the one clock that was left in the kitchen and realised there was no time left at all. They were due at the Cussock Theatre in fourteen minutes.

The Greatest Showparrot

Claudette had only invited a talonful of guests to her rehearsal, so the theatre wasn't busy at all.

Once inside, Ebenezer went up to the royal box, whilst Bethany descended into the stalls, because she wanted to sit with the other children from the orphanage.

Specifically, Bethany wanted to sit with Geoffrey. At this point, their friendship existed pretty much entirely through comic book recommendations.

"Here you go," said Bethany, removing a comic from her backpack. "It's that demon tarantula one I was telling you about."

"Marvellous. In return, I offer you one about a detective, who's disguised as a tortoise," said Geoffrey.

Bethany flicked through a few pages of *D.I. Tortoise: Fast Thinker, Slow Walker,* and immediately decided that she was going to like it. She shoved the comic in her backpack, and changed the topic of conversation to cover the new director of the orphanage.

"What do you think of Timothy then?" she asked.

"Oh, fine, fine. He has an unusual shape of spectacles," said Geoffrey.

Geoffrey was a well-mannered young man who had been raised to always look out for the best in people, even if the best thing one could find was a mildly interesting shape of spectacles. Bethany was maddened by Geoffrey's refusal to speak badly of others.

"I think he's a weak fart who wouldn't be able to lead a mouse to a bit of cheese," she said.

"It would perhaps be useful if he was a little stronger with some of the children – especially Gloria. I'm sure he's trying his best, though," said Geoffrey, who was getting as close as he could to insulting another person.

"What's this Gloria like? Is she worse than me?" asked Bethany, feeling oddly competitive.

By way of response, Geoffrey held up his hands. They were covered with cuts and plasters.

"Gloria made us all sew her a sequin jacket. None of us were very good at using the machine," he explained.

"Why did she want you to make her a sequin jacket?"asked Bethany.

"You'll see in the briefest of moments," said Geoffrey, standing up. "Sorry, but Harold and I have to prepare the smoke machine. We've been forced to help Gloria hijack the rehearsal with a surprise performance."

Geoffrey ran up the aisle and climbed on to the stage – apologising to the rest of the audience as he did so. A row down, a boy by the name of Harold Chicken did the same thing – but without quite so many apologies.

Geoffrey and Harold had been unable to find a smoke machine at such short notice, so they improvised by setting a couple of newspapers on fire and running around the front of the curtain. Meanwhile, the rest of the children from the orphanage started drum rolling to announce Gloria's arrival – bashing empty biscuit tins with splintery chopsticks as a substitute for drum kits.

The drum roll grew louder and louder, and the newspaper smoke grew thicker and thicker, until Gloria Cussock marched onto the stage. She was wearing a badly sewn sequin jacket, paired with a top hat that was too big for her and a set of tap shoes which left deep nail marks in the floor. Bethany wanted to shove worms up her nostrils already.

"You lucky, lucky people," began Gloria. Her voice was dripping with affectation, as if every word she spoke had been practised several times in the mirror. "For tonight you will not have just one performance, but two! And I'm so sorry, but mine is going to be *much* better than the parrot's."

She performed a self-written song entitled 'Gloria the Glorious', whilst Geoffrey and Harold ran around the stage fanning away the smoke they had created. It was a song and dance number, where neither the song nor the dance brought any joy to the audience.

"My ears is hurtsing!" said Amy Clue, a toddler from the orphanage who was sat on the other side of where Geoffrey had been sitting. Her review of the performance echoed the feelings of the entire audience.

The song was short but it didn't seem like it, and by the time Gloria reached her finale, Bethany felt like she had spent an entire week sat in the theatre. The applause was far from thunderous.

"You are welcome," said Gloria, as she took a

deep bow. "But, I'm afraid that there will be no encore."

The applause warmed up considerably after Gloria made this announcement. One relieved theatregoer cheered.

"Gloria's even worse than I thought!" Bethany said to Geoffrey, as he came back to his seat.

"Well . . . *cough* . . . at least . . . *coughedy-splutter*. . . she's . . . *cough*fident," said Geoffrey.

Gloria left the stage, and Mr and Mrs Cussock entered it. They both looked about as interesting and theatrical as a yoghurt pot.

"We're sorry about Gloria and her *unscheduled* performance. She may be our daughter, but I can assure you that we do not consider her part of the family. Please do not judge us, or the Cussock Theatre School, by what you have just seen," said Mr Cussock.

"My husband is quite right," agreed Mrs Cussock, in a voice that was just as dull as Mr Cussock's. "Now, as you all know, tonight is a mere rehearsal for Friday's show. Our establishment is a champion of ground-breaking and immersive theatre, but this is our first time welcoming a singing parrot to the stage. I'd like to offer personal apologies, but absolutely no refunds, if this proves to be awful. Please welcome Claudette to the stage."

Mr and Mrs Cussock exited. The curtain slowly drew open to reveal Claudette, perched upon a bar stool and wearing a fabulous feather boa. Under the gaze of the spotlights, the sleeplessness was clearer on Claudette's face, and, even though it couldn't be possible, Bethany thought that she had lost quite a bit of weight since the morning.

"Good evening, poppets, and welcome to *The Patrick Extravaganza*! Thank you all for letting me rehearse in front of you – it's frightfully decent of you," said Claudette. She didn't seem remotely bothered by the fact that she was following the worst warm-up acts in the history of theatre. "The songs you are about to hear tonight were all performed or written by my dear cousin Patrick – one of the finest parrots who ever lived. Patrick died in this very neighbourhood a month ago today, and this concert is to mark his memory. He lived a good and happy life, and all of tonight's songs will reflect that."

Bethany glanced up at the royal box and watched Ebenezer squirm with guilt.

"I've never done a show like this before, but there was a voice inside my head telling me that I simply had to give it a go. It just wouldn't shut up. Anyhoo, that's quite enough talking – let's crack on with the music!" said Claudette, before bursting into a particularly jazzy rendition of ABBA's 'Summer Night City'.

Claudette moved seamlessly through the rehearsals, singing songs from Patrick's life and punctuating the time in between with moving and amusing anecdotes about the times she had spent with her cousin. She was a talented performer, as demonstrated by the fact that the small crowd rose to give her a standing ovation at the end of every song.

"Oh poppets, you are far too kind," said Claudette, as she came towards the end. She was utterly delighted by the happy faces that were shining back at her "Sadly, it's almost time for me to leave you. For the grand finale, I plan on singing a fun little number that Patrick wrote whilst he was on tour with The Beatles. It's my favourite song of his, and, whenever I hear it, I always feel like I could do anything in the world."

The song was indeed a rather fun and toe-tapping number. It was called 'Hurricane Picnic', and it had a chorus that was catchy enough for everyone in the theatre to sing.

"The Hurricane's here, oh but not for us
When I have you near, oh there is no fuss
Let's dance a waltz love, and sing to our song
Lay out the best mat, click the kettle on
Nothing can hurt us, 'cause we're together
Let this hurricane go on forever"

Bethany did not join in with the singing, because she was very much not a singer. Nevertheless, by the time Claudette came to the end of the song, everyone was calling for her to sing it all over again.

"Gosh, how very nice of you all, Patrick would be delighted. I suppose we have time for one more – are you sure you want the same one? I know plenty of other songs," said Claudette.

"More Hurricane! More Hurricane!" roared everyone in the audience.

Claudette beamed at the crowd again. But then, as she was beaming, Gloria started pulling Harold Chicken's hair and telling him off for giving Claudette bigger claps than her. The sight of such unkindness seemed to affect Claudette deeply. Her left eye began to twitch.

"More Hurricane! More Hurricane!" the audience roared again.

Claudette looked away from the hair-pulling Gloria. She took a gulp of water, cleared her throat, and started again, but this time something went wrong.

The first note out of her beak was neither fun nor toe-tapping. It sounded like cats scraping paws down a blackboard. Bethany had heard Claudette sing several songs, and she had never known her to miss a note.

"Frightfully sorry," said Claudette. Her voice was weak, and she was swaying on her claws. "Let's try again."

Claudette didn't get a chance to try again, because she fainted off the bar stool. The green velvet curtains closed quickly in front of her.

The Snazzy Barnacle

Bethany and Ebenezer ran backstage. Claudette lay unconscious behind the curtain, whilst Mr and Mrs Cussock peered over her in a questioning manner. Bethany pulled out a catapult from her backpack, loaded it with a rotten tomato, and pointed it at the Cussocks.

"Who did this to her?" she asked. "Show yourself, or I will show you the true meaning of pain."

No one stepped forward. No one was shown the true meaning of pain.

"I think she just collapsed," said Ebenezer.

"Perhaps it's all part of the performance," suggested Mr Cussock. "There are many plays where the principal character dies at the end of the show. Although it's a little unusual to see it happening in a singing concert."

"More Hurricane! More Hurricane!" roared the remains of the audience on the other side of the curtain.

"Should we . . . oh, I don't know . . . call someone or something?" asked Mrs Cussock.

Before anyone had time to call someone or something, Claudette woke up. She stumbled to her talons and looked around the stage. Her eyes were filled with fear and uncertainty.

"What happened?" she asked.

"Still investigating," said Bethany. She waved her catapult threateningly around the stage.

"You fell over. Maybe the encore was too much for you?" said Mr Cussock.

"No, that can't be it. Wintlorian parrots are always ready to sing another song," said Claudette.

"Or maybe you haven't had enough to eat?" suggested Ebenezer.

Hope flittered into Claudette's eyes.

"Well, the only thing I've eaten recently is a banana. I flew here straight from the bird-keeper's, and he didn't offer me so much as a worm to eat. Bethany, would you mind awfully if I . . . ?" asked Claudette, looking hopefully at the rotten tomato.

Bethany unloaded the catapult and chucked the tomato in the air. Claudette caught it in her beak and ate it with a single gulp. A little colour returned to her pale, purple cheeks.

"Can I get you anything else? Water? Plasters? Some ice for your head?" asked Bethany.

"Oh, don't worry about that. I'm feeling much better now, I promise," said Claudette. "There's no need to make a fuss."

"More Hurricane! More Hurricane!" roared the impatient audience.

Claudette hobbled over to the curtain, but Mrs Cussock held her back. "I don't think you're ready for any more songs," she said.

"But there's no one else who can finish the show," said Claudette.

Right on cue, Gloria made her grand return to the stage, determined to give the small crowd what they didn't want. Bethany and the others heard Gloria clear her throat on the other side of the curtain.

"Everyone, I have the most wonderful news!" shouted Gloria in her affected voice. "I have literally *just* written a brand-new song. It's called . . .'Tornado Snacktime'!"

'Tornado Snacktime' was a rip-off of 'Hurricane Picnic', and not a very good one at that. Gloria screeched and tap-danced her way through the number, causing people to flee for the doors as fast at their legs could carry them.

When she finally took her bow, there wasn't a single person left in the audience, but Gloria didn't notice. She walked through the curtain to join Bethany and the others.

"Wasn't that just marvellous?" said Gloria. "Did you see my standing ovation?"

"That wasn't a standing ovation, that was people getting up to leave," said Bethany.

Gloria gave Bethany a nasty stare. She didn't appreciate negative feedback.

"Give me that catapult," said Gloria. "I'm gonna use it as a prop in the next show I put on at the orphanage."

"Bog off, bog breath," said Bethany, as she grasped the catapult tighter.

Gloria Cussock was not used to taking no, or indeed 'Bog off, bog breath', for an answer. She put her hands on her hips, bent her knobbly knees, and started scraping her tap shoes along the floor – creating a deeply unpleasant noise as she tore up bits of the stage.

"Gaah!" said Bethany. She dropped the catapult as she

hastily shoved her fingers in her ears. Gloria scooped it up and grinned triumphantly.

"I *always* get what I want," said Gloria. She turned to her parents. "What did you think of my performance, Mummy and Daddy?"

"Please don't call us that!" barked Mr Cussock.

"And that performance was your worst yet!" added Mrs Cussock.

Gloria looked momentarily wounded by her parents' remarks, and Claudette's left eye twitched again at the sight of such unkindness. "My next one will be much better – you'll see!" she shouted, as she ran back through the curtains in pursuit of the other orphans.

"Excuse Gloria, she's an embarrassment to the family," said Mr Cussock. "We should never have had children."

"Yes, let's move on to less repellent things," said Mrs Cussock. "Claudette, we actually enjoyed your performance. It came as a great shock to us both."

"We also feel that it could make a great deal of money. Would you be willing to spend the next three days doing a bit more to promote the show?" said Mr Cussock.

Claudette shook her head. The Cussocks' lips curled in nasty unison.

"Oh deary, no. I'd much rather keep the concert small – not much bigger than this evening's rehearsal, ideally," said Claudette. "I wouldn't know what to do with a whole theatre full of people. That sort of thing was much more suited to Patrick."

"But—" began Mr Cussock.

"No buts. If she doesn't wanna do it, then it's not gonna happen," said Bethany. "Come on, Claudette, let's get you home."

Bethany, Ebenezer and Claudette left the theatre and zoomed off in the car. Bethany and Ebenezer sat in the front, whilst Claudette perched on the roof.

"I'll never get used to this place," said Claudette, when they reached the fifteen-storey house. "It's so beautiful it makes a parrot like me want to spend the whole evening saying things like 'Whoa!' and 'Gosh!'"

"It used to be more beautiful, before you made us sell all the good stuff," grumbled Ebenezer.

"Well, I think there are still plenty of beautiful things in the house," said Claudette. "Take that shirt you're wearing – it's one of the prettiest things I've seen! Have you worn it around me before?"

Ebenezer had felt uncomfortable wearing the shirt, ever

since *The Patrick Extravaganza* had begun. The exquisite softness of the beast's gift made his skin itch with guilt.

"You definitely haven't seen it," he said.

"Hmm, how strange. Somehow, I feel like I recognise it," said Claudette.

Bethany quickly got to work, preparing sandwiches for everyone. She was at an early stage in her sandwich-making career, and her recipes were best described as 'experimental'.

"Here you go," she said, laying the plates on the table. "On the left we have mustard and marmalade, in the middle there's a round of paprika and marmite, and on the right we have the new and improved squashed-muffin recipe – those ones are Ebenezer's favourite."

Bethany wrongly believed that Ebenezer was a great fan of her sandwiches. He was often the first sampler of the fillings, and he was used to finding at least two out of every three new recipes to be inedible. Claudette, however, seemed to feel differently – she gulped down sandwich after sandwich, cooing happily as she swallowed each one.

"Frightfully sorry, chaps, I've almost eaten the lot of them!" said Claudette.

Bethany was delighted to see her sandwiches go down

so well, and Ebenezer was delighted to see them go. They both told Claudette to finish them off.

"Mmmnh, absolutely spiffing!" said Claudette. Her belly was round by the end of her feast. "You really are an incredibly talented young girl, Bethany."

Bethany grinned with pride, and then yawned with exhaustion. The day of de-beasting, do-gooding, theatre-going and sandwich-making was catching up with her.

"Can't be bothered to go upstairs. I'm gonna sleep on the sofa again," said Bethany.

"Don't be silly, I'll carry you up. Grab hold of my talons," said Claudette.

"Are you sure you're strong enough after all that fainting stuff?" asked Bethany.

"Oh, I'll be fine. Those sandwiches should give me enough strength for several days."

Claudette hovered above Bethany's head, so that her talons were in the optimum grabbing position.

"Night, Ebenezer," said Bethany, with another yawn.

"Goodnight, Bethany," said Ebenezer.

Claudette looked at Ebenezer, whilst Bethany was dangling from her talons. "I don't know why, but I really can't shake the feeling that I've seen that shirt somewhere before," she said, before flying Bethany up to her room.

This was the last straw. Whilst Claudette sang Bethany a lullaby, Ebenezer removed the shirt and replaced it with one from the laundry basket.

It seemed a pity to throw such a beautiful garment away, so he went over to the Barnacles' house and prodded the bell. Eduardo opened the door, sipping from a mug of luxurious hot chocolate.

"One more item from the sale," said Ebenezer, as he handed over the shirt. "It's self-washing, and made from the world's finest materials."

Eduardo took a few deep sniffs of the shirt. "This is very fine, Mr Tweezer, but I'm afraid it is a little too large for me," he said.

"Just put it on. It'll fix itself," said Ebenezer. He held the hot chocolate whilst Eduardo tried on the shirt. It started out far too baggy, but shrank around Eduardo's body so that it soon looked like it had been tailor-made for him.

"This is much better than the other things I purchased," said Eduardo. "That diamond-encrusted cheeseboard somehow made all the cheese mouldy, and *not* in a good way, whilst that ducky of yours sings really depressing songs. I was going to enquire about refunds, but this more than makes up for it."

"Good. The shirt's more precious than both those things combined, so I'll be keeping this hot chocolate as well," said Ebenezer.

He ignored Eduardo's pleas of 'HEY!' and 'I SAY, SIR!', and headed back to the house to finish off the hot chocolate in the company of a Victoria sponge. But as he sat in the comfort of the grand sitting room's grandest armchair, he couldn't shake the feeling that he had experienced when he handed over the shirt.

It was strange (ludicrous, even), but as he gave the shirt to Eduardo, he could have sworn that the shirt looked angry – as if it was furious about the fact that Ebenezer had given it away.

"Don't be ridiculous," Ebenezer said to himself. "Shirts don't have feelings!"

The Precious Vomit

That night, Ebenezer's dreams were haunted by memories. In the last of these memories, he was sitting in the beast's attic, dabbing his dry eyes with an exquisitely embroidered handkerchief.

"I still don't understand why you asked me to vomit out that ridiculous thing," said the beast.

"It was for the funeral," said Ebenezer, woundedly. "And it was a jolly good funeral too. Well, not good . . . and certainly not jolly. But, you know, there was a lot of dashed respectful crying going on. I think Nicholas would have been very pleased."

"My dear boy, I think he would have been a lot more pleased if he hadn't accidentally impaled himself on his own pointy stick," said the beast. "He was a moron, unworthy of mourning. You should have let me puddle him, all those years ago."

"He always loved making those pointy sticks . . ." said Ebenezer.

Even though their relationship had got off to a rocky (and pointed sticky) start, Ebenezer had spent more time chatting with Nicholas than any other human. This was because he had made Nicholas spend every Saturday afternoon with him, using the threat of the beast as a motivating influence.

Under the circumstances, it was hardly surprising that the conversation had been somewhat stilted. In spite of this, Ebenezer was still determined to feel poopy when he died.

"Come now, Ebenezer. Your attempts at misery are bringing down my mood. Would you like me to vomit out some jazzy trousers or something?" asked the beast.

"I don't think that's going to help," Ebenezer said. It was the first time he'd ever had a problem that couldn't be at least partially solved by jazzy trousers. "The thing that upsets me most is the fact that I'll never spend another awkward afternoon with Nicholas again. They were the highlights of my week, even though I'm pretty sure they were the lowlights of his. I just can't get my head around how someone can be here one day and then gone the next."

"It's called death, Ebenezer. It happens to all stupid people."

Ebenezer dabbed again. This time, mainly in an attempt to show the beast that its comments were most unhelpful.

"Oh fine then," said the beast, with a stinky sigh. "If I vomit out a way for you to see him one more time, will you perk up?"

Ebenezer nodded eagerly. The beast closed its three black eyes and shut its dribbling mouth. It started to wiggle its blob of a body and made a low humming noise as it moved from side to side.

Then, all of a sudden – Ebenezer woke up.

It had been centuries since he'd thought about Nicholas, and the generous gift that the beast had vomited out. As he got dressed and went downstairs, he tried to figure out why the memory was revisiting him.

The radio was on in the kitchen, and the neighbourhood radio station was playing 'Hurricane Picnic' on repeat, because everyone who had been at the rehearsal was calling in to request it. Claudette was dancing and singing along – her face beaming with pleasure – but Bethany was just dancing, because she refused to sing in front of Claudette.

Ebenezer joined them. His singing was adequate, but his dancing was absolutely terrible – all arms and legs, with no sense of rhythm. He crashed into the saucepans during one particularly ambitious move.

"What are you doing you stupid gitface?" said Bethany. She was laughing at him, whilst the politer Claudette attempted to keep a straight face.

"Letting loose like it's 1899. And I must say, it's far more invigorating than the usual morning bath," said Ebenezer. "You should give it a go. Sing along with us!"

"No way. I am not a singer," said Bethany. But she was drowned out by the sound of Ebenezer and Claudette singing loudly over her.

The three of them continued to boogie on down until the station finally went against popular demand and played a different song. Ebenezer walked over to the table, and found that his place had been set by Bethany. The knife and fork were the wrong way round and her napkin swan looked like a sat-on seagull, but she had thoughtfully laid out his favourite comic. It wasn't quite a magical gift from an all-powerful creature, but Ebenezer appreciated it nonetheless.

"Right then, poppets, what do you two fancy this morning?" asked Claudette.

She insisted on making breakfast every morning, as a way of saying thank you to Ebenezer and Bethany for letting her stay at the fifteen-storey house. Like all Wintlorian purple-breasted parrots, she had the ability to lay eggs containing any type of food, and Ebenezer was constantly testing her.

"Caviar on toast with some Himalayan truffles sprinkled on top," he said, convinced he'd outwitted her this time.

Claudette nodded, jumped up and down twice, and gave her bottom a shake. Ten seconds later, she laid a shiny blue egg, which she gave to Ebenezer.

"Here you go," she said, with a beaky smirk.

Ebenezer cracked it open on his plate, and out popped a portion of caviar on toast with Himalayan truffles sprinkled on top. He took a tentative nibble, and found it was amongst the best he had ever tasted. Claudette laid an egg filled with pains au chocolat for Bethany, which went down similarly well.

"You're flipping amazing! Can you lay me a comic to read as well?" asked Bethany.

"No can do, I'm afraid. Remember, we parrots can only lay food," said Claudette.

"My beast used to be able to vomit out anything in the world," said Ebenezer.

He spoke without thinking about what he was saying. Bethany and Claudette looked at him in a horrified fashion.

"I hardly think that the beast is a suitable topic for the breakfast table," said Claudette.

"No, it's flipping well not!" said Bethany.

"Sorry. I had a good dream last night," said Ebenezer. He thought about the beast's gift again, and whether it might still be somewhere in the house. "I mean, nightmare. I had a terrible nightmare."

"Oh, I had one of those as well. I was in a different body, and I couldn't stop laughing at someone who was crying in pain," said Claudette. "It's most peculiar, because I'm most sensitive to anyone being treated badly or unkindly. Anyhoo, all nonsense really. How was your sleep, Bethany?"

"Fine," said Bethany. She was disappointed to be the only one without a nightmare to report. "Nothing but snores."

"Lucky you. Now, tell me, what do you two have planned for the day?" asked Claudette.

"More do-gooding, I suppose," said Bethany.

Ebenezer groaned, whilst Claudette beamed and asked what do-gooding Bethany had in mind.

"Dunno," said Bethany. "We've tried drinking soup and washing clothes, but that didn't work. Any ideas?"

"Well, you can't go far wrong with volunteering," said Claudette.

"Voluwhating?" asked Ebenezer.

"Volunteering. It's when you offer to do bits and bobs for your community," said Claudette.

"What's the point of that?" asked Ebenezer.

"I'm not sure there is a point, but it's always good to help people," said Claudette.

"I think it's an awesome idea!" said Bethany. "Let's call it *The Beastly Volunteering*!"

"No, absolutely not. There will be no more mention of the beast to people outside this house," said Ebenezer. "Remember what I told you about that secret organisation that hunts for beasts. They could be anywhere."

"Even if they were on our doorstep it wouldn't matter, you idiot. Because the beast isn't here anymore," said Bethany.

"I could still get into a lot of trouble for having hidden it in the house," said Ebenezer.

"That's a load of nonsense," said Bethany. "There's probably not even such a thing as a secret —"

She was interrupted by a knock at the door. Ebenezer gulped.

"Nah, it can't be," said Bethany.

She and Claudette went to the door, whilst Ebenezer made the decision to hide under the table. When they got there, there were no secret agents at all. It was just the lizard-looking lady who worked at the zoo. She was holding the scooter she'd picked up from the yard sale, and she looked

deeply unhappy.

"I knew it was too good to be true," croaked the lizard lady. Her eyebrows were arched in an 'I knew it was too good to be true' sort of manner. "From the moment I heard you were involved, Bethany, I knew the sale would bring nothing but trouble. I don't know why I let Eduardo convince me of anything otherwise – I still remember that day you gave laxative to the elephants."

"What are you talking about?" asked Bethany.

"We were shovelling their poop for days, that's what I'm talking about."

"I meant the scooter, not the prank. Didn't the chimpanzees enjoy riding on it?"

"You know full well that they didn't. I don't know what trickery you did, but the scooter keeps throwing them off it. The poor things."

"There must be some mistake. Bethany didn't do anything to that scooter," said Claudette. "Is there any possibility that the chimpanzees might be to blame for their poor scootering?"

"Don't you dare try and put this on the chimpanzees!" croaked the lizard lady. "I know Bethany organised the sale to pull pranks. How else do you explain all that?"

Bethany and Claudette had to walk on to the front lawn in order to see the 'all that'. They found that several things had been returned to them from the beastly yard sale. Many of them came with notes accusing Bethany of having pulled nasty tricks on them.

The self-decorating Christmas tree had been returned, because once inside the milkman's home, it had started redecorating his whole house, with no sense of style or panache. The televisions had all been returned because they refused to play any channel other than *Tractor TV 24/7,* whilst the astronaut suit had been brought back by the librarian, because it kept mooning visitors.

"I don't understand what happened," said Claudette.

"Bethany happened," said the lizard lady. "Everyone would be better off keeping well away from her." And with that, she left the fifteen-storey house.

Bethany was quiet as she and Claudette brought the things into the house. Once they were inside, and once Ebenezer had extricated himself from the table, Claudette explained what had happened.

"You could have warned us about those things, Ebenezer," said Claudette. "People are blaming Bethany for their behaviour – it's awful to watch!"

"There was nothing to warn you about. They were all nice and useful, when the beast vomited them out for me," said Ebenezer. "Eduardo said similar strange things happened to his stuff as well . . . it's almost as if the presents are angry at being given away to other people. But that can't be possible, can it?"

Bethany couldn't give a rat's jumper about why the beastly things were behaving in such a strange manner. "They all think it's my fault," she said, quietly. "It doesn't matter what I do, they all see me as evil."

"Don't be downhearted, poppet. People are always slow to have their minds changed," said Claudette.

"Well, we're gonna speed them up," said Bethany.

"Come on, we're going volunteering. Right away. That'll show those suckers how wrong they are about me."

She grabbed her backpack and headed for the door. Claudette flew after her, but Ebenezer remained behind.

"You too, gitface," said Bethany. "You can start at the old people's home. You love looking at other people's wrinkles."

"But I've barely touched my breakfast. Can't I do the voluwhatting another time?" asked Ebenezer.

Bethany was about to tell him that he could do nothing of the sort, because she was determined to drag him into being a good person as well – whether he liked it or not – but Claudette got there first.

"Let's leave Ebenezer to himself. There's no point waistcoating for him," said Claudette, her left eye blinking like a twitch. "I mean, *waiting* for him. Besides, we might get more done if we split up."

Bethany still wasn't happy, but she trusted Claudette, so she didn't kick up a fuss. They left the house, leaving Ebenezer alone with his breakfast.

His thoughts returned to the beast's gift. He was certain that he hadn't seen it at the yard sale. Then, he thought about what Claudette had said, whilst her eyes were all blinky.

"Waistcoating!" he said to himself. "Of course!"

He ran up to the waistcoat wing on the thirteenth floor, and headed straight for the leopard-print section. Hidden underneath a cluttered rail of fabulous patterns, there was a box of things which Bethany and Claudette had missed.

One of the items in the box was the beast's gift. It was a magical memory book that let you see the person you missed most in the world, by turning memories into portraits.

Ebenezer had last used the book to look up his cat, Lord Tibbles. There hadn't been anyone in his life, since then, whom he had missed.

He blew away the centuries of dust and cradled the book in his hands. He hesitated before opening it, because he was afraid of who he might find inside.

The Unwanted Assistance

Claudette and Bethany began their volunteering mission at the bird shop. Like nearly everyone else in the neighbourhood that morning, the bird-keeper was humming the melody to 'Hurricane Picnic'.

"Morning!" boomed Bethany. "How can I help?"

"Ain't that the question what I'm supposed to ask?" said the bird-keeper.

"Maybe on a normal day, but this is no normal day. I'm here to volunteer," said Bethany. "Would you like me to feed a grape to the Fantastically Ferocious Eagle? I can even give that stinky Hoatzin a bath if you'd like."

The bird-keeper was a straight-talking, straight-thinking kind of businessman, and it took him a while to understand the concept of volunteering. His confusion wasn't helped by the fact that he had spent most of the morning resolving a tense argument between Keith the Dove and the Hawaiian honeycreepers.

"I ain't getting it," he said. "You're telling me that you wanna do work here, but you don't want money for it?"

The bird-keeper couldn't believe his good fortune, and he nearly started jumping for joy. But then he almost did a few cartwheels of frustration.

"My bloomin' luck. I get my very first volunteer, and it turns out to be a prankster," he said, grumpily.

"I've given up the pranking," said Bethany. "Gimme something to do. You won't regret it."

"I won't regret it, 'cause I won't do it," said the bird-keeper. "And there's no point lying. Those things you sold me show you're still a nasty prankster."

"Oh deary, not your things as well. What's happened?" asked Claudette.

"The mind-reading vacuum is a menace. I've had to lock it away, 'cause I caught it trying to hoover up the toucans," said the bird-keeper. "Meanwhile, that bleedin' piano in the corner has started playing itself – loudly and 'orridly, when I'm tryna get the day birds off to sleep. It's got Bethany's name all over it."

"But I didn't do anything," said Bethany, sadly.

"I don't believe you, and even if I did, I wouldn't take the risk. My business is too important," said the bird-keeper. "What 'bout you, Claudette – feeling any perkier?"

"All fine," she said, quickly.

"You sure? Your colour don't look right. Let's do some more tests," said the bird-keeper.

"What tests?" asked Bethany.

"Oh, I came here before last night's rehearsal. Just wanted to check that those sleepless nights I've been having weren't anything to worry about," said Claudette, still speaking hurriedly. "It doesn't matter. The results showed I'm an incredibly healthy parrot, didn't they? No more tests for me."

"Suit yourself," said the bird-keeper, with a huff. "Now, if you don't mind, some of us have a business to run . . ."

Bethany and Claudette left the shop. They flew over to the Cussock Theatre to volunteer her services.

"The theatre is no place for children!" said Mr Cussock.

"Especially ones like you! We still remember the day you put superglue on all our seats!" added Mrs Cussock.

The response was much the same when they flew over

to the zoo. Bethany offered to scoop up the elephant's poop for a week, as a way of making up for her previous laxative-related prank, but the lizard lady wasn't having any of it.

"I'd rather sleep a night in the lion enclosure," she croaked. "There's no way I'm giving you access to that much excrement. You'd probably do something horrid with it – I know how prankster minds work!"

"Really, honestly, I'm just trying to—" began Bethany.

"Try it elsewhere, missy!" said the lizard lady. She handed Bethany a lifetime ban notice, and closed her shutters.

Bethany turned to Claudette. "How on earth can I be expected to do good if people won't let me help them?" she moaned.

"I can't believe how frightfully unfriendly people are proving," said Claudette. Her left eye twitched again at the unpleasantness of it all. "Don't worry though, poppet, I'm sure something will turn up. Where shall we go next? What about that gentleman with the gold teeth I saw you speaking to at the yard sale?"

"Nah, Jared Kettlefletch is the last person who'll help me become a do-gooder. I can only think of one other place," said Bethany.

The place was the orphanage. Once again, Bethany's offer of help was met with a distinct lack of enthusiasm.

"Are you serious?!" whispered Timothy. As they sat in his office, Bethany and Claudette could hear children wailing and screaming outside.

"Yeah," Bethany whispered back. "I've spent most of my life here, so you won't have to show me around. There's gotta be loads I can help with."

"Another child is the last thing this place needs! Especially a troublemaker like you," said Timothy. "With your parents, it's no wonder you turned out so difficult. I've read your file, you know."

"My file?!" whispered Bethany. She fumbled in her back pocket, and produced the picture of the moustachioed man, and the moustacheless lady. "Tell me everything you know about my parents now, or I'll show you real trouble."

Timothy frowned at the photograph.

"Oh, are those your parents? They look charming. It must have been someone else's file," whispered Timothy. "I've had to read an awful lot of them. Do you have any idea how many children there are here?"

"Let Bethany help you then," whispered Claudette. "I bet my feathers you won't regret it."

"Absolutely not. I don't see how this place would benefit from bringing in a prankster who thinks it's a good idea to give Gloria Cussock a catapult," whispered Timothy. He refused to listen to Bethany's claims that the catapult was, in fact, stolen. "Gloria's been terrorising the children. Every time she hits one of them, she calls it 'method acting.' Thank goodness she hasn't found me yet."

"I just wanna do some good. *Please,*" whispered Bethany, desperately.

"NO!" shouted Timothy. He covered his mouth and looked nervously at the door.

Bethany and Claudette left Timothy shaking with fear. By this point, Bethany was feeling completely miserable about the whole volunteering mission.

As they were leaving the orphanage, they found Gloria towering over Geoffrey. The catapult was loaded with a mushed apple.

"Oi!" said Bethany. "Get away from my friend!"

Gloria turned to face Bethany. She was still wearing the tap shoes, but she had exchanged the sequin jacket and top hat for a ballgown and tiara.

"Can't you see that I'm rehearsing? After last night's triumph, I'm going to hijack Friday's show as well," said

Gloria. "My new song's called 'Cussock the Catapulter', and I'm *trying* to get into character."

Claudette opened her beak to protest. Gloria reached over and snapped it shut.

"Shh, shh, there's no need to say anything. I know how grateful you must be," she said. "As my payment, I'll only take *half* the profits you were going to donate to the orphanage."

She turned back around, and aimed the mushed apple at Geoffrey.

"Why don't you go catapult Timothy instead? He's hiding in his office," said Bethany.

"An excellent idea," said Gloria. "I'll do that next."

Gloria catapulted the apple into Geoffrey's face, and tapped her way towards the building. Bethany helped Geoffrey to his feet and used the sleeve of her jumper to wipe away the apple. The two of them looked at each other. Neither of them knew what to say, without having a comic to start the conversation.

"I'm going to go hide in the washing machine," said Geoffrey.

"Try the space behind the fridge. She'll never find you there," said Bethany.

Geoffrey followed her advice, whilst Bethany and Claudette continued their exit from the orphanage. Bethany didn't know how much patience she had left.

"Let's stop at Miss Muddle's on the way home. You deserve some sweets after today," said Claudette.

"I dunno if sweets are gonna help. If even the orphanage won't take me, how am I ever gonna become a better person?" said Bethany. "It feels like nobody in the world trusts me."

Bethany looked over, expecting a word or two of sympathy from Claudette, but a strange change seemed to have come over the parrot. All the other times Claudette had seen unkindness recently, she'd seemed physically wounded, but now there was a strange smirk upon her beak – as if some part of her was pleased about what had happened.

Her twitching eye was flickering from sparkling blue to shiny black.

The Unexpected Spot of Do-Gooding

Whilst Bethany and Claudette were flying around the neighbourhood, Ebenezer was looking at pictures of himself. Specifically, he was looking at pictures of himself with the beast.

The first of these images was a portrait of Ebenezer and the beast at The Frost Fair, which had been held on the neighbourhood's frozen lake, during a particularly cruel winter. Ebenezer was not much older than thirty, and the beast was still small enough to be transported around the place in a basket, with three carefully carved out eyeholes.

In the background, behind one of the ice-skating jesters, Ebenezer could make out the face of Nicholas Nickle the

Second. He had been a horrid child, who inherited his late father's penchant for making sticks of the excessively pointy variety.

The next portrait showed Ebenezer and the beast pouring a chamber pot of pee-pee over the smug, bewigged head of Nicholas Nickles the Eighth. The one after that recalled the occasion, around the time of Nicholas Nickles the Thirteenth, when the beast had reluctantly agreed to waltz with Ebenezer to save them both the bother of attending the neighbourhood ball.

There were portraits of items that the beast had vomited out over the centuries. Many of these had been sold in the sale, but there were some, like the rocket wellies and the smooth-talking spatulas, that must have still been lurking in one of the house's many hidden spaces.

The book was a real page-turner, and it could be read over and over again, because the memories changed every time Ebenezer went back to the beginning. He was so caught up in his own past that he didn't stop to think about what it all meant.

But, just as he was about to commence his fourth reading, he realised what the memory book was really showing him. It suggested that the person Ebenezer missed most in the world was . . . the beast.

"Oh no," said Ebenezer. Then just to make his stance perfectly clear, he added, "Oh no, no, no!"

He couldn't believe it was possible. It was one thing to think that his life ran a little smoother when he had a magical creature around, but it was something else to be actually missing the slobbery, murderous menace.

Reluctantly, Ebenezer closed the book – knowing that he really shouldn't look at it any more. He took it downstairs and hid it under the sofa in one of the sitting rooms, because he wasn't ready to return it to the land of leopard-print waistcoats.

He tried distracting himself by going outside to deal with the beastly items that had been added to the lawn. When he opened the door, he found an extraordinarily old man squinting at the objects.

"Can I help?" asked Ebenezer, in a way that really said 'Get off my lawn, strange old man!' He said it again, louder, because he saw that the man's hearing aids were switched off.

"Hmm?" said the old man. He was supporting himself with two walking sticks. "Oh, hello there. Can you help me?"

"That's literally what I just asked," said Ebenezer,

testily. The memory book had left him in a thoroughly disagreeable mood. "What are you doing here?"

The old man fiddled with his hearing aids. "I'm here for the yard sale," he said, in a ragged and jangly voice. "Dorris told me there were some wonderful things to be had."

"Dorris? Who the heck is Dorris?" said Ebenezer. "The yard sale was yesterday. Done, gone – finito. We sold everything."

The old man raised an eyebrow at the objects on the lawn.

"You won't want any of those," said Ebenezer. "They've all been causing mischief."

The old man's face fell, and Ebenezer felt a rush of pity. Then he had a sudden surge of inspiration, as he remembered Bethany suggesting that he should do a spot of voluwhatting at the old people's home. It felt like an opportunity to do something similar had landed, quite literally, on his doorstep.

"Would you like to come inside? You know, rest your legs and that sort of thing?" asked Ebenezer.

"My legs do not need a rest!" said the old man, defensively. All the same, he started waddling with his walking sticks to the front door. "But a cup of tea would be delightful."

Ebenezer went back into the house. He boiled the kettle,

laid out his third best tea set, and brewed the perfect pot of purple tea. When he walked over with the tray, he found that the old man still hadn't made it past the front door.

"Here, let me help you," said Ebenezer.

"I do not need any help!" said the old man. "I'm going slowly by choice."

The old man finally passed the threshold. He held out one of his sticks, as if offering Ebenezer a handshake.

"The name's Mr Clinke," said the old man.

"And mine's Ebenezer Tweezer."

"Ebenezer Squeezer?"

"No. Tweezer. TWUH-EEE-ZERRR!" shouted Ebenezer.

"There's no need to shout," said the old man. "I heard you perfectly well the first time."

The old man squinted around the house. Then he squinted at Ebenezer.

"You're awfully young to live alone in a house like this," said the old man.

"I actually live here with a child and a parrot. I used to live here with some . . . *thing* else, but that's all over now," said Ebenezer.

"Some*thing*? Was it a pet?"

"Oh, it was so much more than a pet. It's been my one

and only companion for the majority of my life, and . . . and, yes. I probably shouldn't say anything else about it."

"Young people talk such nonsense," said the old man. He waved one of his sticks dismissively in the air. "I can barely understand a word of what you say."

"Sorry. Well then, shall we have some tea?" said Ebenezer. "If you'd like, there are some sandwiches in the fridge. But, I'd advise strongly against them."

"Aren't you going to offer me a tour first?" asked the old man. "You young people have no manners whatsoever."

"It's fifteen floors," said Ebenezer, looking pointedly at the walking sticks. "And there's no elevator."

"So?" said the old man, defensively.

Ebenezer didn't have the heart to protest, so he put down the tea tray, and led the old man upstairs. The journey was long and yawnworthy, because it took the old man ages to climb each flight.

The old man squinted at each room, and made various unkind remarks about the decoration tastes favoured by 'you young people.' He even demanded to be shown into the cold, cabbagey attic, which Ebenezer hadn't visited since the beast had been eaten.

"This is even worse than the rest of it," said the old

man. "I have much better taste than this!"

Ebenezer felt strangely protective of the beast's old room, and he was going to say something in defence of the damp, dreary style of decoration. But then he realised it would be much better to move the conversation on entirely.

"Do you live nearby?" he asked, with a tight smile.

"I'm currently at the retirement home," said the old man, speaking as if he were confessing to some terribly shameful secret. "It's not because I need to be there, mind you! It's just that . . . well, it's what's easiest for me right now."

"There's nothing wrong living in a—" began Ebenezer.

"I never said there was!" said the old man, crossly. He

removed some used tissue from his pockets and started blowing his veiny nose. "It's just a temporary measure. Dorris will come and get me soon enough."

"Is Dorris your wife?" asked Ebenezer.

"Yes, I am sort of married to Dorris," answered the old man. "I was hoping to pick up a little something for Dorris from this yard sale of yours. Silly old me, for missing it."

The old man's eyes welled up with frustration.

"Don't worry, Mr Clinke. I'll find you something," said Ebenezer, feeling oddly sorry for this odd old man. "Something far better than all that junk that's out there on the lawn."

Ebenezer went downstairs and fished among his things for something Dorris might like. In a great feat of generosity, he donated the teapot from his fifth favourite tea set. Just as he was putting it to one side, the doorbell rang.

Ebenezer found a distressed looking nurse on the other side of it. She wore a nametag reading 'MINDY.'

"So sorry to bother you, sir, but I don't suppose you've seen an elderly gentleman? He's about this tall, and answers to the name Mr Clinke?" she asked, somewhat breathlessly. "He's our newest resident, and I'm afraid he's not taking well to the retirement home life."

"Mr Clinke is just on his way downstairs now," said Ebenezer. "He should be about two hours."

Nurse Mindy's face lit up with relief, when she saw the old man – who was much quicker going downstairs than he had been going up them. Ebenezer handed over the teapot, and received a grateful, wrinkly smile in return.

"Thank you, Squeezer," said the old man. "You young people are . . . so kind, I don't know what I'd do without you."

He waddled out towards Nurse Mindy's car – angrily refusing all her attempts at help along the way. Ebenezer stayed on the doorstep to wave them goodbye.

He felt a warm, fuzzy, do-goody sort of feeling – one that had been absent from the soup-drinking and clothes-washing attempts. He felt he deserved a reward for his do-gooding behaviour, and he thought that one more teeny tiny look at the memory book wouldn't hurt anyone.

He was still thinking about his do-goodery, when he opened the book. He glanced down and saw an image of the beast snarling at him – as if it was furious with Ebenezer for his do-gooding behaviour.

The Flying Parrot

Claudette's left eye was still shining black when they got to the sweet shop, but she was no longer smirking strangely. She seemed to be back to her normal self.

"You mustn't let the rejections get to you," she said to Bethany. "This is all just a small hiccup – I promise."

The sweet shop was mostly empty, but it was throbbing with noise – because heavy metal music was blaring, booming and rattling from the speakers. The young, blue-haired Miss Muddle was hunched over a worktop, trying to inject a miniaturised chocolate bar into a strawberry. She looked up from her experiment in a confused fashion.

"Oh, jingling jelly babies, you're here! I was hoping to save your sweets as a surprise for Friday," said Miss

Muddle, blinking at Claudette through her safety goggles.

"Sweets? What sweets?" asked Claudette, as Miss Muddle led them into her laboratory.

"Why, the ones for your show of course! The Cussocks commissioned me this morning, because they thought some themed treats might help ticket sales," said Miss Muddle. She removed a flour-coated sheet from a table, and showed off her creations. "Sooo, what do you think?"

The table was groaning from the weight of all the sweets on display. There were lollipop trees, which resembled the Wintlorian forest where Claudette and Patrick had grown up, and Elvis-shaped bonbons to mark the time that Patrick had spent on tour with the king. There was even going to be a sweet to reflect the jaunty joy of 'Hurricane Picnic', because Miss Muddle was halfway through swirling some vats of frozen candy floss into the shapes of hurricanes.

"This is all wonderful, but it's far too much," said Claudette, rubbing her talons nervously together. "I really want to keep the show as small as possible."

Miss Muddle was too caught up in showing off her wares to take notice. She opened up a jar of purple gobstoppers (decorated with cartoonish pictures of Patrick's face), and offered them to Bethany and Claudette.

"I rolled these in a variation of popping candy," she explained. "Most popping candy is designed to fizzle your tongue, but this one does fizzly things to your ears instead. When I get them right, they should make you feel like you've just heard someone sing a beautiful song. I thought I'd give them out to the audience after the show – so they can suck on them whenever they want to think about the concert again."

Bethany and Claudette tried the gobstoppers, and true to Miss Muddle's words they both felt a pleasing tingle in their ears – the sort of feeling you experience when you hear someone sing live.

"Thank you, Miss Muddle," said Claudette. "It's all far more than I was expecting, but . . . well, Patrick would love it."

"Why *did* you come here?" asked Miss Muddle. She knitted her blue brows at Bethany. "Hold on a hot strawbooble, aren't you the one who put a frog into my jar of liquorice lemon drops?"

Once again, Bethany's pranking past had caught up with her. She tugged at one of Claudette's wings and went to leave the shop.

"Bethany's much better now," said Claudette, refusing

to go. "And she's been looking for a chance to prove herself. We came to get some cheer-me-up sweets, because she's spent the whole day getting rejected by the neighbourhood."

"Looking to do a spot of good, are you? What kind of thing did you have in mind, Bethany?"

"*Anything*," said Bethany. The emotion of the rejection-filled day was making her voice all wobbly. "I just wanna try and do some good for once, but no one trusts me."

"Well, I'm not surprised, if you've been hiding frogs around the place. I could have lost my shop if the health inspector had decided to visit on that day," said Miss Muddle. She tried to pull a stern face, but it quickly tumbled into laughter. "I must admit, it did amuse me, though. You should have seen the frog hopping about the place, during its sugar rush. He was quite literally bouncing off the ceiling."

Bethany smiled weakly. Miss Muddle stared at her, sizing her up as if she was a new, sweet-related ingredient.

"If you do really want to help, and if you're happy to cease all the froggy business, then I might have something. Everyone deserves another chance . . ." she said, leading them back into the main part of the shop.

The sweet-maker led them to a pile of hand-wrapped

food hampers, which were piled under the candy-cane clock. They were split into groups labelled:

Retirement Home,

Children's Hospital and

Orphanage.

"A new project of mine I'm about to launch – I'm making some little picnics for those who need it most," said Miss Muddle. "I don't suppose you'd be willing to lend me a hand, Bethany?"

Bethany's face lit up with excitement. After such a long, trying day, she couldn't believe that someone was finally willing to trust her.

"And perhaps, in return for your help, I can offer you an education in the art of sweet-making?" said Miss Muddle.

The sweet-maker smiled when she saw the excitement on Bethany's face. She grabbed her ladder and took it over to the bookshelves that were stacked above the till. She climbed to the top and brought down a book entitled *Quantum Mechanics for Morons*.

"Now then, you need to know all sorts of things if

you want to be a proper sweet-maker. Read the first chapter of this tonight, and come back for the night shift tomorrow," said Miss Muddle. "You can help me deliver the first load of packages. Go on then – off you pop. And please take a complimentary bag of the jazzy beans on your way out."

Bethany left the shop, coming dangerously close to skipping for the first time in her life. She clung on to the copy of *Quantum Mechanics for Morons* as if it were her favourite teddy bear.

"This is it!" she said. "This is the chance I need!"

"Congratulations!" said Claudette. "I knew we'd find someone kind enough to trust you in the end."

"It's much more than that," said Bethany. "When the rest of the neighbourhood sees me delivering those packages, they'll all realise how wrong they were, and they'll start trusting me too. I'll make sure of it."

"Whoop-whoopedy-whoop! I'm so very happy for you," said Claudette, and her black eye started flickering back to blue. "We should celebrate with some . . . whoa, whoa – hey, stop that!"

Claudette was talking to her wings, which had started to flap without her consent. She looked fearfully at them and tried to grab the floor with her talons, as she began to take off.

"Claudette? CLAUDETTE?" shouted Bethany, as the parrot disappeared into the clouds.

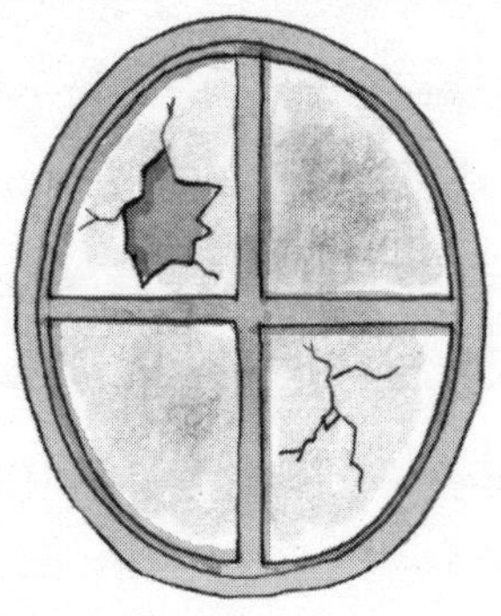

The Broken Window

Ebenezer slammed the book shut. When he opened it again, the beast's snarl was replaced with another 'happy' image of Ebenezer and the beast hosting a well-mannered Peruvian bear in the attic. In the memory, Ebenezer and the bear were conducting a heated debate on the topic of winter footwear, whilst the beast was keeping the party going by vomiting out party games aplenty.

Ebenezer closed and opened the book again and again, but the snarl never returned to the pages. There was nothing but the supposedly 'happy' times that Ebenezer had spent with the beast, and he began to wonder whether there had ever been a snarl there at all.

As Ebenezer looked closer at the portraits, he noticed

that all the memories were incomplete. For instance, the portraits didn't show how the beast had fireballed the Frost Fair when it had got jealous of Ebenezer talking with other people, and the portraits revealed absolutely nothing about what had happened to the poor bear, after they finished that last game of Twister.

This was most unlike the memory book. Whenever it had previously shown Ebenezer images of the person he missed most in the world, the memories were always bad ones.

When Ebenezer had used it to look up Nicholas Nickle (the First), he saw all the times the Nickles had bullied him, and when he used it for the late Lord Tibbles, the book showed him the cat scratching the sofa, or bringing half-dead birds into the house.

At the time, it felt like the beast had vomited out the book just to show Ebenezer that he was better off without other people in his life. But now he wasn't sure, because the book was rewriting the beast as a charming, generous, and rather gorgeous creature.

"Where are the rest of the memories?" said Ebenezer. "The *real* ones."

In response, the book showed him another pleasing

memory involving a hook-handed penguin, a tap-dancing giraffe, and an oddly nimble statue of Winston Churchill.

Ebenezer threw the book across the room. The book flew back across the room and struck him on the head.

"OWW!" said Ebenezer.

The book bounced onto the floor. Ebenezer swore he saw another image of the beast snarling, but when he looked again there was just another 'happy' beastly memory. Ebenezer chased after the book and flicked through it.

Whilst he was flicking, the front door opened. He yelped, and quickly threw the book under the chair.

He straightened his outfit, and stood, trying to look as normal as possible. Bethany burst in, carrying *Quantum Mechanics for Morons* under her arms. She searched the room, before settling her eyes on Ebenezer.

"Claudette?" she said.

"Ebenezer, actually," he replied, nonchalantly. He fervently hoped that the memory book wasn't peeking out from under the chair. "You don't find a parrot wearing this sort of cravat."

"Don't be a twit," said Bethany. "We need to find her. She flew away from me, and I can't find her anywhere. I've been looking for flipping ages."

“Maybe you should just take the hint. Sounds like she’s wanting a little Claudette time,” said Ebenezer.

Bethany walked over and kicked Ebenezer in the shins, repeatedly. The kicking only stopped when they were interrupted by a scream and an almighty smashing of glass, which came from the front room. They both ran to see what was happening, and found Claudette lying face down in a pool of window shards, with a small plastic bag lying next to her.

"Claudette!" cried Bethany, running over.

Claudette rolled onto her back. She was blinking in and out of consciousness, like someone emerging from a dream.

"Bethany? I . . . I'm . . . where am I?" The parrot sat up, and looked around her. As she spoke, she sounded like someone trying to remember another person's shopping list. "I flew here, didn't I? Yes. That's it, I can see it now . . . I left you at Miss Muddle's . . . and then I flew around the neighbourhood. I went to check something at the Cussock Theatre . . . and then I went to the lake, because I wanted to see the frogs . . . But, why did I want to see the frogs?"

"You've got concussion," said Ebenezer. He glanced back to make sure that the memory book hadn't followed them into the room. "Just take it easy until you can think clearly."

"But I'm thinking clearer than I have done in ages," said Claudette. She shook her head, as if to clear her mind from dust. "All that stuff I just told you about – when I think about it, I feel like I'm rifling through another person's life. I can barely understand why I went to any of those places. Honestly, I've never been interested in frogs in my life. Am I making any sense?"

"Not much," said Ebenezer. "Probably the concussion."

"Would a sandwich make you feel better?" asked Bethany.

"I doubt it," said Ebenezer. He corrected himself, when he saw the hurt look on Bethany's face. "I mean, because she's had a nasty shock. Food will be the last thing on her mind."

"No. Actually, a sandwich is just what I need. I wonder if I could suggest a filling of my own?" asked Claudette. She used her talons to open the small plastic bag that was next to her. It was filled with wiggling worms. "I remember now. After the lake, I got these from the bird-keeper in exchange for a free ticket to Friday's show."

"You want me to make you a worm sandwich?" asked Bethany. She hadn't made a sandwich with live fillings before, and she wasn't keen to start now.

"I know it's a strange request. I was most surprised when I felt myself craving it," said Claudette. "If it makes you uncomfortable, you don't have to do it."

Bethany didn't want to be rude, especially given the state that Claudette was in, so she made the sandwich. This proved challenging, as she wasn't used to dealing with fillings that wiggled away.

She served Claudette the worm sandwich, and prepared

a round of squashed muffin and mayos for her and Ebenezer – taking extra care not to confuse the plates. Claudette devoured hers in one bite.

"Did that taste OK?" asked Bethany.

"Extremely edible. It seems that I'm *loving* the taste of raw meat at the moment," said Claudette, mopping her beak with one of her wings. She seemed much perkier now. "And it's reminded me of something important. Whilst I was flying around, I gave some thought to your trust problem with the neighbourhood, and I think I've got an idea that'll involve lots of sandwiches."

Bethany leant in to listen closer.

"We need to give you a new public image. Instead of Bethany the Prankster, we want people in the neighbourhood to see you as Bethany the Kind and Helpful," said Claudette. "And what better way to do that than through an apology party?"

"What on earth is an apology party?" asked Ebenezer. In all his 512 years of existence, he had never heard anything like it.

"It does exactly as it says on the tin – at least I think it does, anyway. You invite everyone who you've pranked or hurt in some way, and give them mountains of food whilst you apologise and show them how you've changed as a person," said Claudette.

"I LOVE it!" said Bethany.

"Yes, it's a good idea, isn't it?" said Claudette. She looked fearfully at Bethany and Ebenezer, as if she was scared by the brilliance of her own idea. "Funny though, because I can't remember coming up with it. In fact, I can't remember having ever heard of an apology party before. It's like when I thought of putting on *The Patrick Extravaganza* – I just don't know where these ideas are coming from."

"Lots of good ideas often come about as a bit of a surprise," said Ebenezer. "Some of my finest cravat and shirt combinations have come out of nowhere."

"Let's do the party tomorrow! I'll get cracking on the invitations," said Bethany.

Bethany headed up to the stationery suite on the seventh floor and brought back down everything she needed. She settled upon a glittery blue card as the most appropriate choice for an apology party.

"Where are the fake moustaches? The ones we used on our last bucket-list day?" she asked Ebenezer. "I wanna give the invites some personality."

"They're in my room," said Ebenezer, who had been

using them to see if he could make a pair of trousers more interesting. "I'll get them now."

Ebenezer went up to his room, but he was stopped in his tracks before he could go hunting for moustaches. The memory book was lying on his bed, and it was shining with a look of triumph.

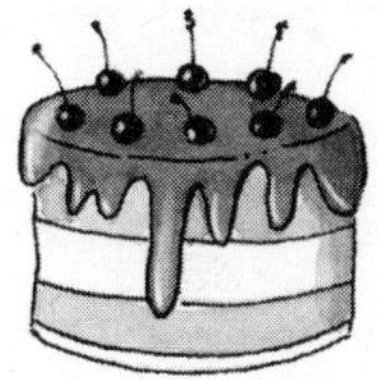

The Runny Sausage

Ebenezer did not have a good night's sleep, because his attempts at slumber were constantly interrupted. No matter where he put the memory book, whether under the tombs in the Egyptian mummy suite or locked in the exotic tea pantry, it always found a way back to his bedroom.

The book didn't do anything to hurt Ebenezer, but it didn't do anything to put him at rest either. It insisted on reminding him of the beast – showing edited highlights of their time together, and reminding him of all the gifts that had been vomited out over the centuries. The more the book tried to rewrite the past, the more Ebenezer relived the horrors of his real life with the beast.

Eventually, Ebenezer could take it no more. He went

downstairs, but found that he wasn't the only one up at an early hour.

Bethany was hard at work preparing for the apology party, and she had already moved onto the sandwich section of proceedings. It seemed that every ingredient in the house was out on display; jars of pickled turnips lurked ominously next to overripe avocados, and there was a mixing pot on the go, which contained a foul-smelling mixture of plum jam, mayonnaise, ketchup, treacle, brown sauce, and honey. Ebenezer dreaded to think what sort of sandwich abominations would be made by the end of the day.

"How's it going?" he asked.

"Awesomely. I'm making fourteen different types of sandwiches, all the fizzy drinks are in the fridge, and I've got everything I need to lay the table," said Bethany. "Everyone's gonna let us do so much do-gooding by the end of this party, it'll be flipping ridiculous."

"Us?" asked Ebenezer, groaning inwardly.

"Hell yeah," said Bethany. "Don't think I'm letting you wriggle out of it. I know you didn't go to the retirement home yesterday – your car was in the exact same place."

"As a matter of fact, the retirement home came to

me," said Ebenezer, terribly pleased with himself. He was significantly less pleased with himself when he saw the confused scowl on Bethany's face. "I mean . . . an older gentleman came round. Mr Clinke was his name – a frail, yet fierce sort of fellow. I invited him in, let him criticise the house a bit, gave him a teapot – that sort of thing."

Bethany stopped stirring her pot of menace. She looked up at Ebenezer with a strange expression on her face.

"You actually did some do-gooding? You listened to me?" she asked.

Ebenezer realised that the expression on her face was one of pride. He didn't know what to do with this, because no-one had ever been proud of him before.

"Well . . . um, you know," he said, shuffling awkwardly. "Thought I'd give it a go."

Bethany resumed stirring. The look of pride, quickly gave way to her usual scowl.

"Good start, but, now you gotta take it up to the next level. You need to go to the retirement home today – go and give your company to some other oldies as well," she said.

Ebenezer pulled a face. He rather thought that giving an old man a teapot would cover his do-gooding quota for the year.

"Hold on a mo, this isn't his, is it?" asked Bethany. She fished her pockets and produced an earwax-covered hearing aid. "I found it on the stairs."

"Oh yes, that's Clinke's all right," said Ebenezer, taking it off her.

"Mind if I have the earwax? It smells a bit cheesy, so I thought I could use it in my mozzarella and marzipan recipe," said Bethany. She scooped off the wax and rubbed it into some nearby slices of bread, before Ebenezer could stop her. "It's gonna add a flavour the guests are just gonna love. I can't wait to see their faces."

"Indeed, I imagine they will be pulling all manner of interesting expressions," said Ebenezer. "Who is coming to enjoy these very special sandwiches, by the way?"

"Oops. Good point," said Bethany.

Even though she had spent most of the night preparing the invitations, Bethany hadn't sent them out yet – and she was planning for the party to kick off in the early afternoon, so she'd still have plenty of energy left for her first shift at Miss Muddle's in the evening.

"I can fly the invitations around for you," said Claudette. "I'm going out soon anyway to put up some posters for my show."

Neither Bethany nor Ebenezer had heard her come in. She was looking gaunter, and her left eye had turned black again. In spite of this, she was brimming with confidence. There was a smug smile upon her beak, and she flew into the room as if she owned the place.

She was carrying a bag in her talons that was filled with dozens and dozens of rolled-up purple posters. She took one of them out to show it off.

"Last night, I decided that I don't want it to be a small show after all. What's the point in hiding my talent from the world?" she said.

The poster featured a rather flattering self-portrait of Claudette upon the stage, singing to a crowd of adoring fans. It promised that tomorrow's *The Patrick Extravaganza* would not only be 'SHOCKING', 'CAPTIVATING', and 'A THEATRICAL FEAST', but also that

anyone who didn't buy a ticket would be an 'UTTER MORON WHO DOESN'T DESERVE TO LIVE.'

"What do you think, poppets?" she asked.

"It's a bit aggressive," said Bethany.

"Yes. I can't help but wonder whether it may be a smidge too direct," said Ebenezer.

"You two clearly aren't artists," said Claudette, with a beaky humph. "Now then, lucky ones, who wants some delicious breakfast?"

It was most unlike Claudette to describe her breakfasts as delicious, because she was a humble parrot, but Bethany and Ebenezer were too baffled by the posters to take it up with her. Bethany ordered a slice of chocolate cake, whilst Ebenezer opted for a full English. Sadly, the meal did not live up to its expectations.

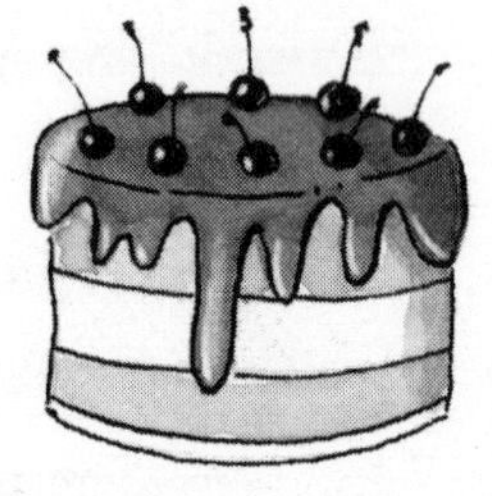

"Is the chocolate cake meant to be stale?" asked Bethany.

"Why are my sausages runny?" asked Ebenezer.

"Maybe next time you should prepare your own breakfasts!" snapped Claudette.

Bethany and Ebenezer knew that they had been a little rude, so they both mumbled apologies and returned to their disgusting food. After a while, they both pushed their plates away, whilst their stomachs made pained, hungry groans.

"Many people would pay buckets for my wonderful breakfasts," said Claudette. She shook her head, like a nervous twitch, and her snappy tone vanished just as quickly as it had appeared. "Sorry, just a bit tired, I think. Right then, I better get started with these posters and invitations. Where are they going?"

"These ones to the orphanage, this one to the bird-keeper, this to the Cussocks, and these to the zoo," said Bethany. "Want me to come help you with them?"

"No!" said Claudette. She raised a wing to her beak, as if surprised by her own forcefulness. "Sorry, I mean no, *thank you*. I'm sure I'll be quite alright on my own. Much more important for you and Ebenezer to crack on with party things."

"Actually, I'm heading off to the retirement home," said Ebenezer, before adding, with a certain sting of regret; "Do-gooding business."

A strange, angry sort of look came over Claudette's face as she listened to this, and her black eye began to flicker. She collected the invitations and flew out of the door.

"What do you think's up with her?" asked Ebenezer,

once she had gone.

"She's probably just moody from tiredness, like she said," said Bethany. "Right then, much more importantly, what do you think I should do about the seating plan? I'd like Geoffrey to sit next to me, but maybe I should sit next to someone else instead – someone who *hasn't* received an apology yet?"

Ebenezer had never had enough friends to throw a party, let alone one with a seating plan. His advice to Bethany consisted of some oohs, ahhs, and inarticulate mumbles.

"Gonna have to be quicker with your answers, gitface," said Bethany.

"Sit someone else next to you," said Ebenezer. "Ideally the person who you've wronged the most. I don't see why Geoffrey's coming at all, if you've already made things up with him."

Bethany scowled. She ignored his advice, and put Geoffrey next to her.

"Anything else I can do before I go?" asked Ebenezer.

"Nah. Just bog off and leave me to it," said Bethany. "I've seen how you butter bread. You show far too much mercy to the crusts."

Ebenezer grabbed his furriest coat, and headed out

the front door. As he was walking over to his car, he saw Eduardo Barnacle approaching the fifteen-storey house, and approaching it in a strange manner.

The young, well-nostrilled boy was wearing the gold-buttoned shirt. He was walking very strangely – with two outstretched arms, and his feet dragging along the ground, as if he was being pulled towards Ebenezer's house by an invisible thread.

"Help me, Mr Tweezer! Please, get it off me!" shouted Eduardo.

Ebenezer was going to inform Eduardo that he did not care to have his day interrupted by some childish game, but then he noticed that the gold-buttoned shirt seemed to be the thing pulling Eduardo along the street.

"I don't know how you're doing that, but stop it. It's not funny," said Ebenezer.

"It's not me, Mr Tweezer!" said Eduardo, who was now being dragged across Ebenezer's front lawn. "It's the shirt!"

Ebenezer tried to continue on his way to the car, but the shirt kept on using Eduardo to block him. Whichever direction Ebenezer went, Eduardo was dragged there to stop him.

"Look, I don't know if you're lonely or something – but

please let me get to my car. I'm trying to do some do-gooding," said Ebenezer.

"It looks like the shirt doesn't want you to do anything of the kind. I can assure you I'm hating this just as much as you, Mr Tweezer," said Eduardo, and the angry flaring of his nostrils suggested that he was telling the truth. "This shirt of yours has been nothing short of a nuisance. Every time I put it on, it either tries to strangle me with an overly tight neckline, or the sleeves make me beat myself up. I don't want to wear it any more!"

"And I don't want *you* to have it any more, if this is how you're going to behave with it," said Ebenezer. "You're acting like a fool."

Then, as if it had heard their conversation, the shirt unbuttoned itself from Eduardo's body and flew into Ebenezer's arms. The sleeves wiggled and stroked at Ebenezer's skin, like a needy cat.

"See!" said Eduardo, defiantly. "It wants to be with you. I knew you'd done some sort of trickery to it. You and Bethany were probably in it together!"

Ebenezer looked down at the shirt and wondered whether it was possible for a shirt to be so picky about its owner.

"Well then, Mr Tweezer – how do you explain yourself?" asked Eduardo.

"I think . . . I have absolutely no idea," said Ebenezer.

The Dejumbling

Ebenezer calmed Eduardo down by giving him the money to get a new fancy shirt that wouldn't prove anywhere near as tricky or murderous. His efforts to calm himself down, however, weren't quite as successful.

Ebenezer clutched the shirt, and the shirt clutched at him – as if thrilled to be reunited. He stumbled back into the fifteen-storey house and found Bethany in the grand sitting room, busily folding napkins into sat-on seagulls.

"Bethany, I—" began Ebenezer.

"Thought I told you to bog off," said Bethany. "I'm too busy to chit-chat."

"Yes, I know. It's something important, though."

"More important than getting the rest of the neighbourhood to trust me?"

"Well, I think it might be. Please, just give me a minute."

Bethany stopped seagulling, and looked at him. She tapped her foot impatiently to make it clear that Ebenezer better be saying something good.

"Well, you see – it's about this shirt . . ." began Ebenezer. He didn't have time to finish his thought because Bethany picked up one of the forks and threw it at him.

"A shirt?! You wanna stop me from preparing the most important party that's ever been held anywhere to ask me about an outfit!" she said, angrily throwing another fork. "Get out of here, you selfish git!"

"It's not just the shirt," said Ebenezer, as another fork sailed above his head. "It's also about all those things that came back from the beastly sale, and there's this book I've found that—"

"Now is NOT the time!" said Bethany. "We can chat about how strange the world is after my party. If you don't leave right now, then I'm gonna have to start throwing the knives."

Ebenezer yelped, dropped the gold-buttoned shirt, and ran back out of the house. He jumped in his car and started driving to the retirement home – not knowing what else to do.

As he drove, he saw that Claudette had plastered posters across the whole neighbourhood. There wasn't a street corner, bus stop, postbox, or public lavatory that didn't have Claudette beaming beakily from it.

Ebenezer was so distracted that he took his eyes off the road and almost ran over the kindly old lady again. The lady didn't make a fuss, but a fellow pedestrian shook his fists angrily.

"Open your eyes, you hooligan!" said the pedestrian.

As Ebenezer drove on, he wondered whether he should follow the man's advice – and not just in regard to his driving. If Bethany wasn't going to talk to him until after the party, then maybe he needed to open his eyes and have a proper think about all the peculiar things that were going on.

The shirt, the book, the returned items – they had all been vomited out by the beast, and they were all behaving strangely. This seemed significant to Ebenezer, and he wondered whether the things might be playing up because of the death of their creator.

It was a fine enough theory, but it didn't explain how the items were still able to move about the place. Moreover, it offered absolutely no insight into why the shirt had tried to stop him from doing do-gooding.

Ebenezer honked his horn, thoroughly frustrated by his own confusion. He glanced out of the window and saw that he was already outside the retirement home, and that his frustrated honk had caused Nurse Mindy to emerge from the building.

"Thank goodness you're here. Mr Clinke has been asking after you all day," said Mindy. "He's proving to be one of the trickiest residents we've ever had."

Mindy explained that the old man was not taking to the slow-paced atmosphere of a retirement home existence. He kept breaking out of the place, and whenever he was in his room, he wouldn't stop mumbling about how Dorris should have let him stay in a hotel instead.

"We've tried putting deadlocks on his doors and sealing his windows, but he still keeps getting out," said Mindy. "Could you have a word with him and see if you can calm him down?"

Ebenezer already felt like he had quite enough problems of his own, but he promised he would try and help anyway.

Mindy led him to the old man's door and knocked twice before letting herself in. They found him sitting on his bed – fiddling with his remaining hearing aid. Ebenezer felt terribly sorry for him.

"I think you might need this," said Ebenezer, removing the other hearing aid from his pocket. "My friend removed the wax for you."

The old man snatched the hearing aid back, and squinted grumpily at it.

"Tell your friend to keep their mits off my things, next time," he said.

Ebenezer could see that the old man was in a mood, and he thought it might be best to leave him to it. He went to leave the room, but the old man called him back.

"Wait! Please don't go, Squeezer," he said. "Won't you stay with me for a little while? You're the only person I've met in this whole bally place that doesn't treat me like I'm an idiot."

The old man scrunched his wrinkly brow at Mindy, and she took this as her cue to leave. Ebenezer sat at the room's small table, whilst the old man used his two walking sticks to waddle over.

"Sorry about the temper tantrum, Squeezer. I'm finding this all a lot trickier than I expected," said the old man. "Dorris said it would be easy for me – but it's not at all."

"Oh, I can imagine," said Ebenezer, without much sympathy. He was wondering how quickly he would be able to leave the place, without appearing rude. "Must be quite the rotter."

"You have no idea what it's like," said the old man, waving a stick dismissively. "But I'm glad to see you, Squeezer. Shall we play a game of Word Jumble?"

The old man pointed to an extremely old board game that was sat on the table. The cardboard sides were loose, and the writing was so faded that Ebenezer could barely make out the picture on the box.

"Maybe some other time," said Ebenezer, getting up to go. "I really only came here to drop off the hearing aid."

The old man's face fell.

"Don't be like that. It's just that I've got a lot on my mind, you see," said Ebenezer.

"Oh, I see exactly how it is. Everybody's too busy for Mr Clinke," said the old man.

Ebenezer sighed and sat back in his chair.

"One game," he said. "Then I've got to go."

The old man crinkled his wrinkly lips into a smile, and removed a bag of letter tiles from the cardboard box. The rules were simple; when it was your turn, you had to grab the letters for the very first word that popped into your head, jumble them up, and put them on the board.

The other player then had to try and guess the original word – if they guessed within one minute then they got to keep the letters, and if they didn't then the letters (and points) would go to the jumbler.

Ebenezer had never played the game before, but he took enormously well to it. The first words that popped into his head were 'MEMORY' (which he rearranged as 'MY ROME'), SHIRT ('TRISH'), 'EDUARDO' ('DEAR

DUO') and 'BEAST' ('SEAT B'). He was also successfully able to de-jumble the old man's 'CHOP UR DOG' (clearly 'COUGHDROP'), 'SIR ROD' ('DORRIS'), 'SEE ZEN' ('SNEEZE') and 'SUITES' ('TISSUE').

"Rematch?" said the old man.

"I probably shouldn't," said Ebenezer, glancing at the clock. But then he figured that he might as well, because Bethany wouldn't want him getting in the way of the apologising and partying anyway. "OK. But this is definitely the last one."

It definitely wasn't the last one, because Ebenezer lost that round – and he was determined not to leave on a defeat. The old man won the next game after that as well, but Ebenezer evened the score with a tight, fourth-round victory. It seemed a pity not to stay for a decider.

"How's your wild carrot, by the way?" asked the old man, as he set up the board for the final game. Ebenezer greeted his question with a puzzled look. "You told me yesterday that you lived with one."

"Oh, I see. No, not a wild carrot; a *child* and a *parrot*," said Ebenezer. "They're both fine. The child's throwing a party, the parrot's getting ready for a show."

"A show? Can I come? It's got to be better than whatever's

going on in this place."

"Absolutely. She's now decided that she wants as many people there as possible, so the more the merrier. It's very strange, she's had a complete change of mind about the whole . . ."

Ebenezer's tongue was stopped by his thoughts, as he dwelled upon all of Claudette's strange behaviour. The fainting, the gauntness, the black eyes, the snappy tones, the sudden desire to put on the biggest show the neighbourhood had ever seen . . . all of it happening at the same time that the objects had begun to make mischief.

For the first time, Ebenezer put the two things together, and a horrid, preposterous thought started to grow in his head. If Claudette's mind had changed, then what . . . or who had changed it?

"Sorry, Clinke, I've got to go," he said.

"But you can't go! We haven't finished the game!" said the old man, in a pleading tone.

A few centuries ago, Ebenezer would have given anything to have such a willing game-playing companion, but now he ran out of the building and quickly drove home – way past the speed limit. It was four o'clock when he got back to the house. He headed straight to the grand sitting room to see how the apology party was going. It turned out that the party wasn't going at all.

Bethany was sat amongst a mountain of sandwiches and a river of fizzy drinks. Her cheeks were in her hands and tears were leaking from her eyes.

"I have not had an awesome afternoon," she said.

The Apology Afterparty

"No one showed up, no one called to tell me they weren't coming. I prepared all this food for nothing, and I feel like a flipping idiot. Even Geoffrey . . ." said Bethany, as she crossly brushed the tears from her eyes.

Ebenezer looked around at the slowly ruining sandwiches, the jugs of fizzy orange that were losing their sparkle, and the seagull napkins that would all have to be unfolded and put away. He was distracted from his Claudette concerns, because he couldn't believe that anyone could do this to Bethany, let alone a whole neighbourhood.

"Claudette said they definitely all got their invitations. She's gone now to see what flipping happened," said Bethany. "She thinks that—"

The phone rang, and Bethany leapt over – answering before the first ring had rung.

"Claudette? Oh, hey – it's you. Soz, I was expecting someone else."

Miss Muddle was on the line. Bethany wiped her eyes with her sleeves and tried to put on a cheery voice, even though she was feeling about as poopy as a lamppost that's been attacked by a dog with diarrhoea.

"What time do you want me there for the first shift? I have a LOT of questions about the book, 'cause I barely understood a word of it . . . You what? . . . That wasn't me! I wasn't trying to get you into trouble with the health inspector, I promise! . . . No, really, seriously, I haven't been out of the house today . . . I wouldn't even know where to get that many frogs from . . . Hello? HELLO?!"

Bethany looked at the phone receiver as if it had just tried to bite off her ear. Then, she smashed it against the wall.

"Miss Muddle says I'm never allowed in the sweet shop again," she said, smashing and smashing until there was nothing left but a wire in her hand. "Someone broke in and unleashed an army of frogs in her laboratory, spoiling all her food hampers. She thinks I did it!"

"You didn't, did you?" asked Ebenezer. As soon as the

words were out of his mouth, he wished he could take them back again. "Of course you didn't," he said, way too late. "I know you didn't. It's just that you used to be rather fond of putting frogs in unexpected—"

"You're just like all the others," said Bethany. "If even you don't believe me, then how am I ever gonna—? What's the point in—?"

Claudette flew back into the house. She swooped into the grand sitting room and wrapped Bethany in a feathery hug. She was much better at comforting Bethany, and Ebenezer felt foolish for having suspected her of being anything other than a loyal friend.

"I'm so sorry, poppet," said Claudette.

She tried using her wings to dry Bethany's tears, but Bethany wasn't having any of it. She wriggled out of Claudette's grasp and demanded to be told what everyone had said about her.

"Oh, poppet, you really don't want to know," said Claudette.

"Tell me NOW!" said Bethany.

Claudette looked at Ebenezer, as if pleading with him to help her out. Ebenezer didn't know what he should do.

"Well, poppet," said Claudette, with a resigned sigh.

"The reason no one came is because . . . no one likes you. The bird-keeper, the Cussocks, the zoo, all the children at the orphanage – they dislike you because of the pranks you've pulled in the past. None of them trust you, and they thought that this party was just an excuse for some fresh horridness."

Bethany collapsed into a nearby chair, looking as though she'd been slapped across the face by a large, and extremely unfriendly fish. Ebenezer watched Claudette closely, as she hobbled around the room and seemed to grow angrier and angrier about what had happened.

"It just makes me so cross that they won't give you a chance," said Claudette. "This neighbourhood needs to be taught a lesson . . ."

"This neighbourhood *does* need to be taught a lesson . . ." said Bethany. The fish look vanished from her face, and was replaced with a more determined kind of expression.

"I mean this whole thing makes me question why anyone should bother trying to be good in the first place," said Claudette, shaking her head. "Just look at all these sandwiches . . ."

"I don't wanna touch a single one," said Bethany. "They're all ruined for me."

Claudette felt rather differently. With extraordinary speed, she flew around the table and gulped down every sandwich on offer, before washing them down with a couple of litres of fizzy orange. Ebenezer noticed that her stomach didn't grow larger, like it usually did. It was as though all the food and drink had disappeared somewhere inside her body.

"Mmmnh! Delicious – each and every one," said Claudette, mopping her beak with a wing. "I don't suppose that's much consolation, though, is it, poppet?"

"Nah," said Bethany. "I won't be happy about anything again until I get my revenge."

"Hold on now, Bethany. I'm no expert on this sort of thing, but don't let your anger do something stupid. I've made this mistake before—" began Ebenezer.

"You know what, Ebenezer, you're absolutely right," said Claudette. For a brief moment, Ebenezer was relieved, but then she added, "You're no expert at all."

"What?!" said Ebenezer.

"You don't know what Bethany's going through, and you have no idea what it means to be a good person. Let's not forget that you've spent most of your life hunting down innocent creatures for a glorious, wonderful beast to eat," said Claudette.

"Glorious? Wonderful? Now hang on a minute—" said Ebenezer.

Claudette didn't hang on for even a second.

"Bethany, am I not one of the kindest, and most splendid people you've ever met?" she asked. Bethany nodded her head. "Good, so you should follow my advice when I tell you that you can't let people walk over you any more."

"Claudette, what are you talking about?!" said Ebenezer, flustering about what he should do. He noticed that both her eyes were black and he didn't like the look in either of them. "Revenge isn't going to help anyone!"

"It'll help me feel better," answered Bethany. "Instead of being selfish and thinking about yourself all the time, why don't you just take a flipping minute to think about me?"

"Bethany, I . . . of course I care about how you feel," said Ebenezer.

"Well. Not enough. Not like Claudette does," said Bethany, pulling her backpack over her shoulders. She stormed into the hallway, and collected the scooter that the lizard lady had returned to them. "Claudette is the only one who really cares about me."

Ebenezer opened his mouth, closed it again, then opened

it once more – trying and failing to think about how on earth he could prove to Bethany how much he cared about her. Bethany watched him for a few seconds, willing him to say something, but nothing came out of his mouth. She walked over to the front door.

"One more thing," said Bethany, turning to Claudette. "When you said all the children at the orphanage . . . ?"

"I'm sorry to say that I do mean *all* of them hate you," said Claudette. "Especially that Geoffrey boy who you like so much. Apparently, he only trades comics with you because he's afraid you might shove worms up his nostrils otherwise."

"Even Geoffrey . . ." said Bethany. Her face waivered for a moment, before the determined expression returned. "If people don't think I can be good, then maybe I'll show them just how bad I can be."

"Yes!" shrieked Claudette, her black eyes shining with delight.

"No, no, no!" shouted Ebenezer. "Bethany, wait, that scooter might be dangerous!"

But it was too late. Bethany slammed the front door, and roared the scooter away from the house.

"My, my, – I don't think I've ever seen anyone so fired

up before. One can only imagine what she's going to do to the neighbourhood," said Claudette. "Oh and don't worry about that scooter, dear boy. I've told it to behave itself – for the time being, anyway."

Ebenezer ran out of the front door, but Bethany had already gone, and he had no idea which direction she went. He ran, just as quickly, over to the remains of the phone – grasping at the wire, and thinking about all the numbers he could call if it was still working.

"I've also told all the other things in the attic that they must learn to keep quieter," said Claudette. "They have been ever so naughty – making such a mischief about the place. Then again, I suppose I've been a little naughty myself . . . I didn't really speak to any of the neighbourhood, you know – I just flew around the clouds instead."

Ebenezer towered over Claudette. "What are you talking about?" he asked. By way of response, Claudette hurled up one of the blue, moustachioed invitations.

"It's no wonder the guests didn't arrive," she said. Ebenezer bent down and found the invitation was wrapped around a frog's leg. "Oh, and I may have had a little something to do with the hopping menaces in Miss Muddle's sweet shop. I had to snack upon one or two of them, though, because they looked positively scrumptious."

There was an unpleasant smirk upon Claudette's beak, and the voice she spoke with now was not her own. The voice was soft and slithery and all too familiar to Ebenezer's ears. He stopped towering and started cowering, horrified that his worst suspicions were coming true.

"What's with the face, Ebenezer? I know you've been thinking about me, and I want you to know that I've been thinking about you as well. In fact, I've used this time to think exclusively about you and Bethany. Come give your beast a kiss."

Ebenezer backed away, terrified by the grinning creature that was hobbling towards him. He cried out for help, even though he knew no-one could hear him.

"Don't worry Ebenezer, I'll help you," said the beast, through Claudette's beak. "I'll remove that terrible influence from your life, just like I removed all the others who have tried to come between us. But first, I need her to understand that she's just like me."

"B-B-But how are you here? W-W-What? W-W-Why?" stammered Ebenezer.

"Really, after all this time apart from each other, is that all you have to ask me?" said the beast, shaking Claudette's head in a disappointed fashion. "No 'how are you', or 'what's it like being in a parrot'? Frankly, Ebenezer, I'm disappointed with your conversation skills. Perhaps you need some more time with the wall."

Ebenezer scrabbled backwards upstairs, and the beast hobbled after him. It cocked one of Claudette's ears and waited for a more charming line of conversation to present itself. Ebenezer didn't say a thing, so the beast sighed through Claudette's beak and answered the original conversation starters.

"As for the how and the what; first I ate all the food in her belly – that took me a while, she was a fat parrot. At the moment, I'm destroying her kind, hopeful personality. I've never eaten someone through their insides before – I must do it more often," said the beast. "I was going to creep out through one of her eggs – she could have got rid of me herself that way, if she hadn't been so stupid – but this is so much more fun."

"YOU'RE DESPICABLE!" wailed Ebenezer.

The beast shook Claudette's head again. This was not how it wanted their reunion to go.

"If you can't speak politely, then perhaps you shouldn't speak any more," it said. "Time for you to put your

beautiful shirt back on, I think."

The beast wiggled one of Claudette's talons, and with an almighty whoosh, the gold-buttoned shirt flew to the staircase and hovered menacingly over Ebenezer.

"Y-Y-You won't get away with this," said Ebenezer, with admirable optimism.

"Oh, my dear boy, I think you'll find that I already have," said the beast.

The Late-Night Pranking Emporium

The beast's scooter zoomed at a whizz-cracking pace. Even on its 'medium' setting, Bethany was far quicker than all the cars and motorcycles on the road. She travelled so quickly that the air seemed to bite her skin, and the world around her turned blurry.

Bethany arrived at *The Late-Night Pranking Emporium* about twenty minutes earlier than expected. Jared Kettlefletch greeted her on the doorstep.

"Finally! My little prankster has come home," said Jared, flashing his golden teeth. "I knew you wouldn't be able to stay away for long."

The Late-Night Pranking Emporium was not an ordinary joke shop where parents took their children

to buy catapults and whoopee cushions. It was something decidedly more sinister. As Bethany was ushered in, she was greeted by an entire shelf of screaming dolls.

"Say hello to the bloodcurdling screamers," said Jared Kettlefletch. "Perfect for causing frights in the middle of the night."

"They're disgusting," said Bethany.

"Thank you, kindly," said Jared Kettlefletch. "What horridness are you looking for today?"

Bethany didn't have a specific kind of horridness in mind, so she walked around the shop. She encountered a wall filled with robotic book-destroyers, as well as a collection of booby traps that were designed to do various unpleasant things.

Jared Kettlefletch was attentive to his customers, especially ones like Bethany who needed encouragement towards the art of true nastiness. "Have you considered the demonic dream-lolly?" he asked, as he led Bethany to a sweet box that looked just like any other. "One lick and your victim will have nightmares for weeks."

Bethany shook her head. She needed something nastier than a lolly.

"What are those, over there?" asked Bethany. "They look like some kind of robotic rat."

"Robotic rats they are, but kind they are certainly not," said Jared Kettlefletch, leading her over to them. They had red eyes, and black, metallic bodies. "These are my latest design of the superstinkrats."

"How do they work?" asked Bethany.

"First, you load the rats with a stinkpod of your choice. Then, point them at your target, switch it on by the tail, and watch it go," said Jared Kettlefletch. "The rats scramble up the victim's body and spray out a thick pink puff from their nostrils. They have a range of around five hundred feet, so you don't have to be anywhere near the scene of the crime."

"What if I wanna be near?" asked Bethany. "What if I wanna see it happen?"

Jared Kettlefletch flashed a gold-toothed grin.

"Every set comes with nose pegs," he said. "You can also set the rats to a general setting, if you want to attack more than one person at a time."

Bethany nodded and continued to walk around the shop, where she was shown other cruel concoctions like dung-filled sugar cubes and a wind-up baby-snatcher. Once

BOOGERS
BOOGERS

BOG OFF!
BETHAN
POOT
BAM
POOTS

she had seen every item in the shop, she poked her head into the back room, where she saw a workstation and a collection of empty stink-pods.

"That's where the magic happens. I've just created a delightfully awful blend, which I like to call 'The Fishbone Surprise'," said Jared Kettlefletch.

"Can I have some empty pods?" said Bethany, as her mind worked furiously on a new prank. "I wanna make some of my own odours."

"I thought you might. What you did with those objects at the yard sale was genius. You should have seen what that knife tried to do to some of my customers," said Jared Kettlefletch. He laughed so hard, it looked like he might dislodge a tooth.

"That wasn't —"

"Ah yes of course, very wise. You didn't do it all," said Jared Kettlefletch, tapping his nose, as if he was in on a secret. "And if anyone asks, you certainly didn't get the rats from me, eh? We fellow pranksters have to watch each other's backs."

"Just gimme the empty pods and two bags of rats," said Bethany.

Jared Kettlefletch could tell that Bethany didn't know

much about money, so he charged a ludicrous price. Bethany shoved everything into her backpack, and thought about where she would go first to collect the ingredients for her odious odour.

She jumped on her scooter, and whizzed over to the bird-shop. Usually, the bird-keeper stayed in his shop way into the night, but, on this occasion, Bethany saw the shadowy outline of him and his family having dinner upstairs.

"Well. That makes things easier," said Bethany.

She looked up and down the deserted street, before trying the door. It was unlocked, but, once inside, all the birds in the shop turned to face her. They were like guard-dogs, only with the potential to be much, much noisier.

"Hmm, maybe not quite so easy," said Bethany.

She knew that if a single one of them called, quacked, clucked, or cooed in alarm then the rest of them would join in. She scowled, because she thought it would be impossible to get what she needed, but then the beastly piano started to play a lullaby. It was a deeply soothing tune that caused every bird's eyes to droop – even the nocturnal ones who had just woken up for the night ahead of them.

Bethany probably would have dropped off herself, if her

mind wasn't fired up with hurt and angry feelings. She waited until the room was purring with snores, before searching the room for the Hoatzin cage.

The cage was apart from all the others, because none of the birds could stand to be near the creature's stench. Even asleep, it looked lonely.

"I know what it's like, mate," whispered Bethany, as she pinched the nose peg around her nostrils. She reached into the Hoatzin's cage and put a few of his foul-smelling feathers into her stinkpods. "These other birdies deserve to be punished for treating you like this."

Bethany crept back out of the shop. The sight of the friendless Hoatzin reminded her how she had felt sat alone amongst all those sandwiches. She gripped the handlebars even tighter, as she whizzed over to the zoo.

Irritatingly, the zoo was locked up, and the walls were all taller than the lankiest of lampposts. She was about to turn around and head back to the fifteen-storey house, but then the scooter scooted of its own accord. It sent Bethany zooming towards the outer wall of the elephant enclosure, scooting way too fast for her to even think about jumping off.

Bethany prepared to crash, but the scooter had other

ideas. It blew a raspberry to the rules of gravity and started scaling the zoo wall.

Bethany clung onto the handlebars with all her might, as the scooter led her to the very top of the building. She looked down, wondering how she was going to get to the elephants, when the scooter performed its gravity-defying trick once more, and scaled the inside wall of the zoo.

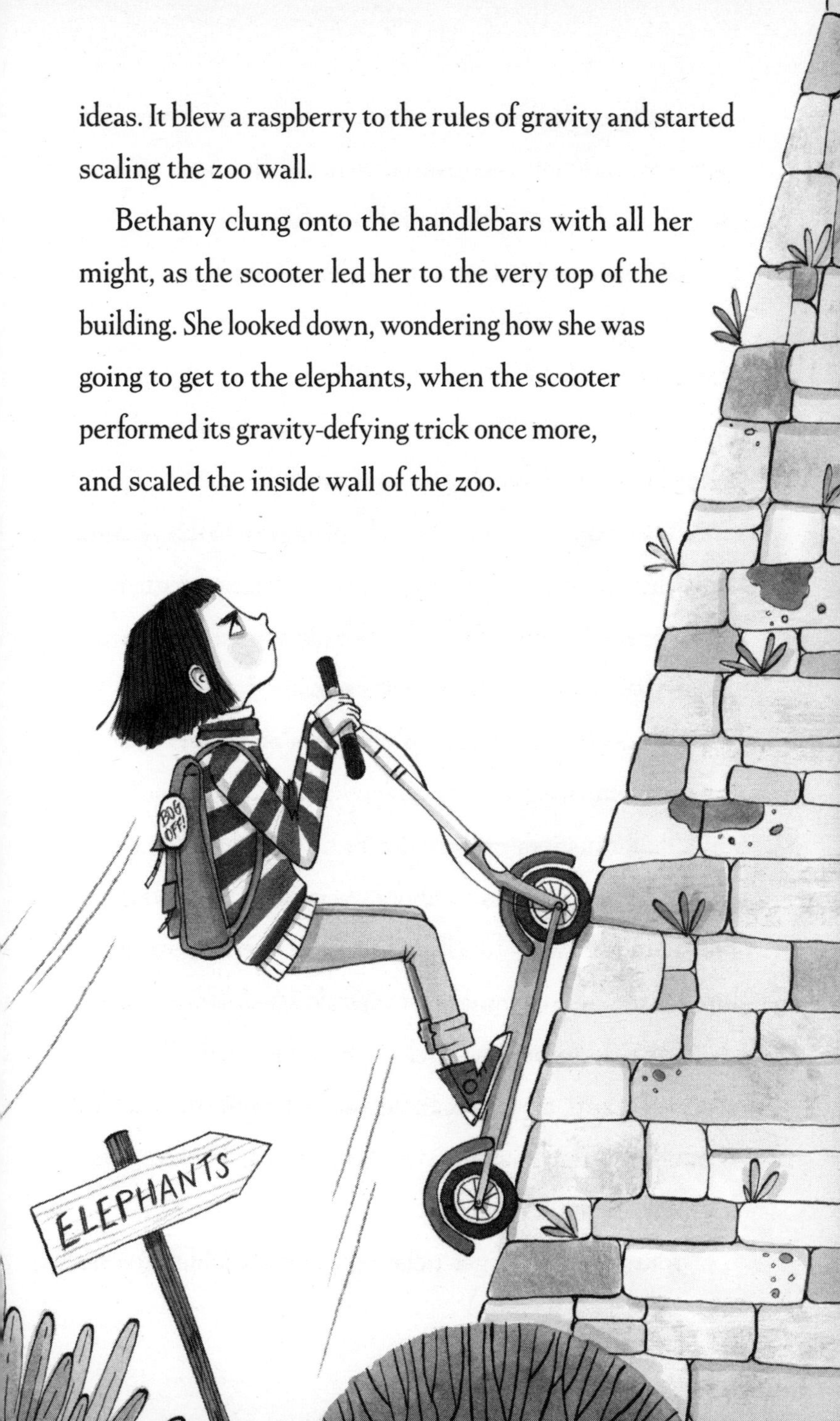

This time, Bethany wisely kept her eyes scrunched shut until she felt the ground beneath her feet. When she opened her eyes, she found herself face to face with a playful baby elephant.

"Hiya," said Bethany.

The baby elephant was thrilled to make Bethany's acquaintance. He lifted up his trunk and returned her 'Hiya' with some bombastic trumpeting.

The trumpeting momentarily deafened Bethany, and drew the attention of the zoo's night-time security guards. Bethany hid behind the baby elephant, whilst the guards shone their lights into the enclosure.

"What do you think's up with this one then?" asked the first security guard.

"Oh. It's just one of the baby ones," said the other older guard. "They get shouty about everything at this stage. He should be fine – we'll just need to keep our eyes on him for the next few nights, that's all."

"Can't do tomorrow night, I'm afraid," said the first security guard, as they walked away from the enclosure. "I'm off to watch that show at the Cussock Theatre. You know, that parrot one."

"You managed to get tickets?!" said the older guard.

"They were sold out when I called. Apparently, it's the biggest show they've done since they staged that one with the dancing magicians . . ."

Bethany stayed behind the baby elephant until the security guards' chatter was far in the distance. Then, she headed over to where the largest pile of elephant poop had piled up.

The smell was far worse than the Hoatzin on his worst day, but Bethany's nose peg blocked all that out. She grabbed some gloves and a nearby shovel, and started carefully shovelling the elephant excrement into a selection of the pods.

She was just returning the pods and nose pegs to her backpack, when she became aware that there were several elephantine eyes upon her. The ground shuddered beneath her feet, as the elephants thumped slowly towards her – all of them seeming to treat her act of poo-thievery as though she had stolen their finest silverware. The baby elephant looked particularly betrayed by Bethany's actions.

"I'm just having a borrow," said Bethany, creeping towards the scooter. "I promise, I'll bring it straight back after I'm done."

This did nothing to please the elephants, and they

thumped towards her with increasing speed, surrounding her like lions around a gazelle. Bethany sprinted towards the scooter. As soon as she'd grabbed hold of it, the scooter took matters into its own handlebars and zoomed Bethany out of the enclosure – weaving her in and out of the battering rams of the elephant trunks, before scaling and descending the wall faster than it had done before.

Bethany zoomed back to the fifteen-storey house. She heard the angry trumpeting of elephants, which in turn, set off a Mexican wave of furious animal noises around the rest of the zoo.

Once these noises were behind her, she congratulated herself on her evening's work. It had all gone far better than expected – and this was in no small part thanks to the surprise assistance that had come from the scooter and the piano.

Bethany wondered why these beastly objects had proved so helpful to her, whilst they had been so unhelpful to the bird-keeper and the lizard lady. She didn't like the feeling that her behaviour was being supported by anything that had had anything to do with the beast, and she began to wonder whether she was doing the right thing.

She thought she should probably have another chat with

Claudette and the selfish gitface about it all. But, when she got home, the selfish gitface was nowhere to be seen.

"Hello, Bethany," said the beast, who was perched on one of the kitchen counters. It spoke with Claudette's sweetest voice. "I'm afraid Ebenezer and I have had a dreadful falling out. He's left the house, and he says he never wants to see or hear from you again."

The Terrible Tweezer

The beast squeezed at Claudette's eyeballs until they watered, and used one of her wings to dab away the 'tears.'

"It was terrible," it said. "I explained to Ebenezer why you need to take revenge on the neighbourhood, but he wouldn't listen. He thinks you're stupid to ask for another chance from the people you pranked in the past. He said that if you think he's selfish, then maybe he'll show you just how selfish he could be."

"Nah," said Bethany. She started looking around the kitchen – opening various cupboards and fridges, convinced that she'd find him hiding in one of them. "He knows I just said those things 'cause I was hurt."

"The only thing he knows is that he wants you and I out of here by Saturday, so he can go back to his wonderful, carefree life of endless bubble baths and tea parties for one," said the beast, squeezing the eyeballs again, for dramatic effect. "I'll have to move on from this neighbourhood, and you . . . well, I guess you're going to have to go back to the orphanage."

The beast wanted to enjoy the look on Bethany's face, but her back was turned, and she spent a few moments just staring intently into a cupboard of biscuits. Then, her spine straightened, and, when she turned around, a part of the cupboard's handle came off in her hand.

"He knows what it was like there for me. He wouldn't . . ."

But, even as she spoke, she didn't believe her own words. There was no way that Claudette would lie to her about such a thing.

She knew that Ebenezer had been struggling with the disruptions to his life, but she never imagined that he would chuck her out. She thought their friendship was more important than that.

Everywhere she turned it seemed like someone was against her. She had begun the day thinking that things were looking up, and she was ending it being homeless, hopeless, Ebenezerless, and consigned to spend her life in the place where she had been so unhappy.

"This is what you get for being a do-gooder," she said. She threw the broken bit of cupboard across the room, causing it to crack one of the fancy teacups that Ebenezer had left out. "I can't go back to the orphanage. Especially, now that I know what they all think about me."

"I don't think you have a choice—" began the beast.

"Stuff that – nobody's ever been very good at telling me what to do. I'm coming with you instead," said Bethany. She looked up, with hope in her eyes. "Please, Claudette, can I? You're the only friend I have left . . ."

The beast had to control every muscle in Claudette's body to stop itself from laughing aloud. Then, it spoke the same words it had used all those centuries ago when it had first met Ebenezer.

"Don't worry, I promise that you will never, ever get rid of me," it said. "I'll take care of you."

The beast felt that this would have been the sort of moment that Claudette might have chosen to hug Bethany. It spread its wings and hopped across the counter, as it tried to figure how hugs worked.

Thankfully, Bethany was in no such hugging mood.

She unzipped her backpack, and laid out the rats and pods on the counter.

"We're probably gonna have to start our new life together after tomorrow's show," said Bethany. "I won't be able to stick around in this neighbourhood, once I've unleashed this particular prank."

The beast grinned – its hold over Claudette strengthened by the promise of such horridness. Bethany wanted to get to work straight away, but her eyes were drooping with exhaustion.

"Actually I might have to wait until tomorrow," said Bethany. "But I promise it'll be worth it."

This irritated the beast, but it tried to appear unaffected by the delay.

"What an excellent idea. I'll fly you up now. Perhaps, I might even sing you a sweet, sweet song at the same time," said the beast.

Bethany grabbed hold of the talons, and the beast started flying a shaky, bumpy route up to Bethany's bedroom. The beast was better at using Claudette's voice than it was at using her wings, but the song it sang was far from sweet, sweet.

The beast hobbled out of Bethany's room, and started

hopping upstairs. Bethany called out, before it could even make the next floor.

"Claudette . . . where are you going?" she shouted.

"What now? You're not expecting a good night kiss or something, are you?" asked the beast.

"No, I was just wondering why you're going upstairs. I thought you were staying in my room," said Bethany, yawning

"I'll join you now, I just need to check on something ahead of the show," said the beast. "Good night."

Bethany shrugged and started snoring on the pillow. The beast flew Claudette's body up the many remaining staircases, and made a note of all the missing objects that would have to be returned to the empty spaces. It summoned the memory book with a wiggle of its talons, and flicked through the pages to remind itself of how the house used to look, before the yard sale.

"Try not to be scared," the beast shouted, once it reached the top floor. "I'd much prefer it if you didn't look scared."

The beast used Claudette's talons to creak open the rickety old door at the top of the stairs. It switched on the light, and ordered the memory book to nestle itself in between the self-decorating Christmas tree, the

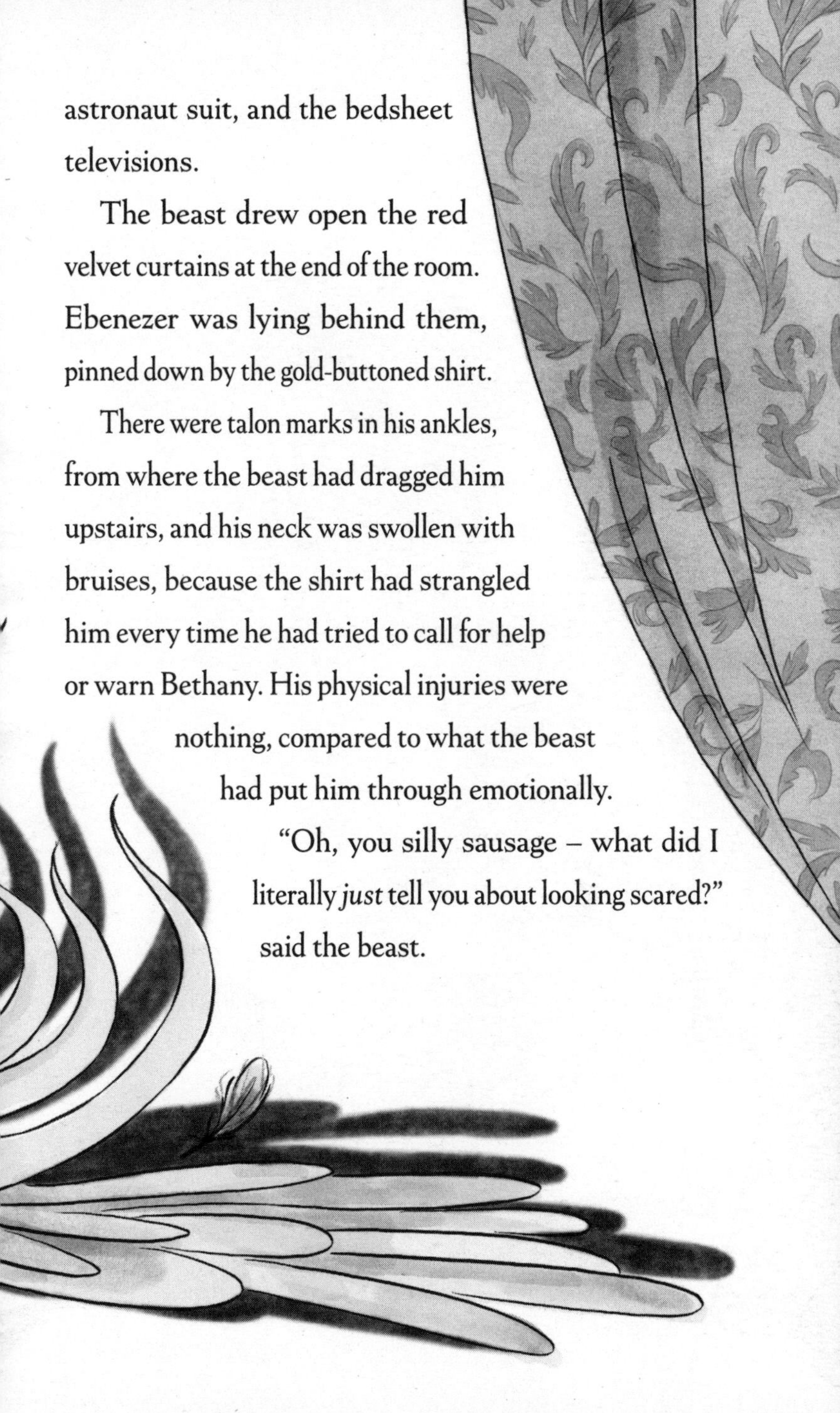

astronaut suit, and the bedsheet televisions.

The beast drew open the red velvet curtains at the end of the room. Ebenezer was lying behind them, pinned down by the gold-buttoned shirt.

There were talon marks in his ankles, from where the beast had dragged him upstairs, and his neck was swollen with bruises, because the shirt had strangled him every time he had tried to call for help or warn Bethany. His physical injuries were nothing, compared to what the beast had put him through emotionally.

"Oh, you silly sausage – what did I literally *just* tell you about looking scared?" said the beast.

The Song of the Beast

"Isn't this a nice change of roles?" said the beast. "Now you're the one trapped up here, whilst I'm free to roam around downstairs and have fun with Bethany."

"What have you done with her?" asked Ebenezer. His voice was croaky from all the strangling.

"I haven't feasted yet, if that's what you're asking," said the beast. "There's way too much fun to be had before all that. Bethany needs to realise that, deep down, she's just as beastly as me."

"Bethany is *nothing* like you!" croaked Ebenezer. He was using his strongest voice, but it barely came out louder than a whisper.

"Oh, I'm not so sure about that," said the beast, as it stretched a wicked little smile across Claudette's beak.

"Let's look at the facts, shall we? Yesterday, she fed me a live-worm sandwich, and today she is planning a horrible revenge for the rest of the neighbourhood. I'm finding it truly empowering to watch her at work."

"Those things are different. She thought Claudette was telling her to do them!"

"Hmm, yes. And I wonder what else she will do if 'Claudette' says it's okay," said the beast. "I've been thinking about that Gloria Cussock who she dislikes so much. Tell me, do you think that I might be able to get Bethany to feed her to me?"

"Don't be absurd. SHE'LL NEVER —" said Ebenezer.

"Tut, tut. 'Never' isn't a very hopeful word now, is it?" said the beast. "Besides, you don't know Bethany like I do. You didn't see how hurt she was when I told her you abandoned her."

Ebenezer couldn't believe that Bethany would believe that he cared so little for their friendship. The beast drank the look of devastation on Ebenezer's face as if it were a delicious blood-cordial.

"Bethany thinks I'm her only real friend left in the world. She thinks I'm the only person who can save her from a life at the orphanage – isn't that hysterical?" said the beast. “And I think she might do just about anything, if I convinced her that Gloria had hurt Claudette in some way.”

“NO!” Ebenezer wrestled against the shirt, and once again lost miserably. The beast shook Claudette’s head disappointedly.

“Hey now, don’t be silly,” it said. “I know why you’re acting like this. You probably think you have to side with Bethany, because I won’t take you back, don’t you? Hmm? Well, you’ll be pleased to hear that I’ve thought a lot about our time together – *before* the unpleasant Bethany blip.”

The beast hobbled over and gently stroked Ebenezer with one of Claudette’s talons. It left a deep cut in his cheek.

“Don’t worry about death, Ebenezer. I know it’s always been your greatest fear,” it said. “Whilst I was plotting my revenge in Claudette’s belly, I thought about what a good servant you’ve been. All the other ones I’ve had grew weak and widdly so quickly, but with you, it took five hundred years before we had any problems. I couldn’t bear to lose such a valuable member of staff.”

“I won’t serve you again,” said Ebenezer. He couldn’t believe he had thought for a moment that he might miss this dreadful creature.

“Yes, you will. After I’ve killed Bethany, all the

unpleasantness will be forgotten, and we'll go back to the old routine," said the beast. "You'll bring me my meals, and I'll give you everything your heart desires. You might be stroppy for a week or two, but you'll get over it – just like you got over your pet cat. What was her name again? Was it Mistress Tibbs?"

"His name was Lord Tibbles, and this is nothing like that! Please, *please* let Bethany go," said Ebenezer. "Give all the punishments to me."

The beast let out a slithery chuckle, and hobbled away from Ebenezer. As it hobbled, feathers fell off Claudette's back.

"Oh no, I've been waiting for this particular dish for quite some time. It's why I've taken time to season the meal, by buttering her up with cruelty and bitterness," said the beast. "My only regret is that you won't be able to see my triumph in person. We must have a little think about how we can involve you in this wonderful event."

The beast hobbled around the attic and had that little think. It stopped hobbling after it was struck by a tremendous idea. The beast wiggled Claudette's talons and made one of the televisions sit in front of Ebenezer.

"I'll film the entire performance and share it to this screen!" said the beast. "In the meantime, to keep you entertained . . ."

The beast vomited a peculiar-shaped wire through Claudette's beak, and used it to connect the memory book to the television. The memories were now video clips.

"Won't it be nice to watch our old life?" asked the beast.

Ebenezer tried shaking his head, but the collar of the gold-buttoned shirt made him nod instead.

"Splendid. Perhaps, after the show, we can throw a little after-show party in my honour?" said the beast. "Would you like to hear the song I plan on performing before I kill her?"

The gold-buttoned shirt made Ebenezer nod again.

"Good, I thought you would," said the beast. "As it's called *The Patrick Extravaganza*, I thought I might sing the last song he ever wrote. Do you know the one I mean, Ebenezer? It was the one he wrote about me, right before I ate him in this very attic."

The beast closed Claudette's eyes. When it opened them again, it imagined that it was performing to a grand audience. It began to sing;

"The beast has the finest house in the land.
It's so tall and long and terribly grand.
Even the Queen, with her palace so wide,
Cannot compete with the beast if she tried."

The tune was surprisingly melodic, because the beast was getting the hang of using Claudette's talents. As the beast sang, Claudette's talons dug into the floor, and moved around leaving strange marks. The beast was too immersed in its own performance to pay any attention.

"The beast has a face, so useful and round.
With three eyes to make sure lost things are found,
And two tongues for licking all it can find,
The beast is quite clearly one of a kind."

The beast bent Claudette's back and took a deep bow at the end of its performance. The arms of the gold-buttoned shirt pulled together to make Ebenezer clap.

"It's amazing what a good song can do for the soul," said the beast. It smiled so wide that it almost cracked a corner off Claudette's beak. "I'll treat you to an encore, when I return."

The beast hobbled towards the door. Ebenezer let out another hoarse cry, but it was no use. He was powerless to save Bethany.

"Oh, and by the way, you'll be having another twenty-four hours without sleep," said the beast, turning Claudette's head around. "Every time you try to rest, the shirt will strangle and squeeze to keep you awake. I do care for you, Ebenezer, but we still need to make sure that you receive some sort of punishment for what you did to me."

The beast shut the door and flew downstairs, enormously pleased with itself. It was so enormously pleased with itself that it didn't notice the exact nature of the marks that Claudette's talons had left on the floor.

The Beastly Duo

Bethany woke up early the following morning, determined to get her revenge ready as quickly as possible. There was no sign of Claudette in her room, so she went downstairs.

Claudette wasn't in the kitchen either, so Bethany was forced to make her own breakfast for the first time in weeks. She switched on the radio, and started beating up some muffins.

She usually loved making squashed muffin sandwiches, but today she found that they reminded her too much of Ebenezer. As she beat up the muffins, she imagined she was beating up him – she even told the muffins that they were morons for sending her away from the fifteen-storey house.

Ebenezer's rejection hurt the most, because he had

been her very first friend. Bethany still wasn't sure how friendship was supposed to work, but she thought they'd been doing a pretty OK job of it, until he had disappeared without so much as a 'See ya!'.

Clearly, she had got it wrong – like she'd got so many things wrong recently.

After breakfast, she turned her attention to the rats, and spent a couple of hours getting her head around the over-wordy manual – figuring out how to load the pods, without causing any of the odious odours to leak out.

In addition to her own Hoatzin feather and elephant poop concoctions, she inspected the scents that had been provided by Jared Kettlefletch. These ranged from the sort of smelly 'Antique Banana' to the thoroughly offensive 'Dead Badger's Fart.' She spent another hour or so, picking out various horrible scents for people.

"Geoffrey's getting a rat for each eye. Serves him right for pretending to be my friend," she said to herself. "Lizard lady's definitely gonna get elephant pooped . . . ooh, and this dead badger one will be perfect for the bird-keeper . . ."

She had also decided that she was going to put a few of the Hoatzin ones on a general setting, so that no one in the theatre would be able to avoid her stinky wrath. The only person left unaccounted for was Miss Muddle.

Miss Muddle was already going to get superstinkratted at the theatre, but Bethany felt that the sweet maker deserved something even better . . . well . . . much, much worse, because she had given Bethany hope and then taken it away.

"Health inspector!" she said to herself.

She ran over to the phonebook. She tore out the page that had the numbers of the health inspectors in the area and shoved into the front pocket of her backpack.

Bethany had expected to feel guilt, or some unpleasantness, as she prepared the pranks, but no such emotions had presented themselves. She didn't just feel marvellous; she felt moreish. She was learning that revenge is the drink that leaves you thirsty, and she was just thinking of what she would do after the show was over, when she heard the front door being opened.

"Claudette!" shouted Bethany, as she ran into the hallway. "Where have you—?"

Bethany was silenced by the sight of Claudette. The beast had bent her beak, so that it was askew, and it had left dark rings of purple around her eyes.

"What happened?" asked Bethany, horrified.

The beast was holding a freshly vomited out silver rope in Claudette's talons. It pretended to limp, as it approached Bethany.

"Gloria Cussock happened," said the beast. It spoke the lie it had been practicing all day. "I was just flying around – doing a few final bits and bobs for the show – when she got me. She said she wanted to be the star of the show, and then she did this to me – so I wouldn't be able to perform. She even tried strangling me with this silver rope!"

Bethany's face fired up with fury. She didn't like Gloria, but she couldn't believe that she was capable of such brutality.

"I'm gonna get her. Three rats in the eye for her – three rats for each eye!" she said, pacing up and down the hallway. "Actually, nah. She deserves much worse than that."

"Oh bother, I don't know about that," said the beast. It treaded carefully, because it knew how close it was to getting what it wanted. "Maybe we should leave it."

"Absolutely flipping not, Claudette!" said Bethany. "We've got to punish her for this."

"Oh dear, oh dear – I hate to be the cause of someone getting hurt," said the beast. It fiddled with Claudette's wings to make it look like it was having a serious think. "Although, I suppose I wouldn't mind it so much if it wasn't just a punishment, but also something which showed her that you can't go around beating up your fellow performers. It would be good to give her a big, nasty shock – one scary enough to change her behaviour."

"Yeah!" said Bethany. "What kind of big and nasty are you thinking?"

The beast sighed through Claudette's beak.

"That's where I'm stumped. Because I'm not really a big, nasty sort of person, you know," it said. "What about you? What's the nastiest thing that's happened in your life?"

"Nearly getting eaten by the beast," said Bethany. "Well, either that, or the time I accidentally stepped on a plug."

The beast made a great show of being surprised by Bethany's answer. It clapped Claudette's wings together in a 'Huzzah!' sort of way.

"Oh that's good!" it said. "You know what, Bethany, I think that might just work!"

"I don't think a plug's gonna cut it," said Bethany.

"No, not the plug, the beastliness! We should eat her," said the beast. "Sorry, I mean, we should let her think she's about to be eaten."

"What?!"

"Yes! That will definitely shock her into changing her ways!"

"But threatening to eat her! How would that even work?"

"Very easily. First, you bring Gloria to the Cussock Theatre – that shouldn't be tricky, you know what she's like. At some point, you bind her hands with this rope. During my performance, I'll pretend I'm about to eat her."

"Then what?" asked Bethany, her mouth drooping open with horrified fascination.

"Well then . . . I obviously *don't* eat her. I'm not the beast," said the beast, letting out a slithery chuckle through Claudette's beak. "Right at the moment it looks like I'm going to peck out one of her eyes, I'll stop and tell her that if she isn't nicer to her fellow performers, I'll hunt her down and eat her for real."

"But Claudette – won't you get in trouble?"

"Don't worry about that. We'll just pretend it's part of the show. The audience will be thrilled, and Gloria will be too terrified to say anything."

"This all feels a bit wicked," said Bethany.

"I know. It's going to be spectacular!" said the beast.

"No, I meant wicked as in, you know, bad and evil."

"What's wicked about it? We're not actually going to do anything to her. It'll just be one big, nasty shock and that's it. I'd say what she did to me was much worse."

The beast made Claudette's face wince with 'pain', and it raised one of her wings to her bruised eyes. Bethany was moved first with pity, and then with renewed fury as she saw what had been done to her only remaining friend in the world.

Gloria needed to be taught a lesson, and Claudette had never been wrong in her advice before, because she was such a kind and wise parrot. Bethany decided to put her squeamishness to one side.

"OK then, if you say it's gonna work, I believe you," she said. "Let's go."

She went in the kitchen, where she shoved the rats and folded the scooter into her backpack. She went to switch off the radio, but then 'Hurricane Picnic' started playing again.

"Switch that off – NOW!" snapped the beast.

Bethany noticed that one of Claudette's eyes was flickering from black to blue.

"But, I thought you loved it. You said that when you hear it, you feel like —"

"I said NOW!" roared the beast.

It hobbled over to the radio – grimacing as it got closer to the noise. Then it crushed the radio between Claudette's talons. In the silence that followed, Claudette's eye went back to black.

"I can't stand that song anymore," said the beast.

"But what about tonight's show?" asked Bethany. "'Hurricane Picnic' was such a good one to end it on."

"Don't you worry, my child. I've got a far more *breath-taking* finale in mind," said the beast. It hovered over Bethany, so that Claudette's talons were in the optimum grabbing position. "Now, shut up and let's get going."

The beast smiled, as it flew Bethany out of the house. This time, the smile actually cracked a corner off Claudette's beak.

The High-Flying Prankster

Bethany was flying high – literally.

She was flying higher than ever before, because the beast was getting cocky in its new body. Usually, Claudette kept close to the ground, because she wanted to keep Bethany safe, but the beast was plagued with no such concerns. It weaved in and out of the soggy clouds, doing occasional twirls, and singing rowdy songs at the top of Claudette's voice.

At this height, the neighbourhood seemed so small, so pathetic – like some kind of toy town that could be crushed at any moment. As Bethany looked upon it, she felt like one of the superheroes from her comics. The people beneath had rejected her, and soon they would realise that they

should have been her friend, not her enemy.

The more she thought about the Gloria idea, the more she liked it too – after all, it was the least she deserved for attacking Claudette. Bethany expected to feel nervous as they travelled to the orphanage, but she felt remarkably excellent.

At this point, the beast dropped her.

It's amazing how a little thing like being dropped from a great height can affect someone's mood. Within moments, Bethany's spirits were no longer riding high, and, as she tumbled through the air, the neighbourhood didn't seem quite so pathetic or toy-townish. It had taken on more terrifyingly life-like dimensions, and she shared her new review of the place by screaming for dear life.

She was just about to be impaled by the pointy roof of the library, when the beast scooped her up with Claudette's talons.

"What the flip did you do that for?" screamed Bethany.

"I thought it would be fun," said the beast.

Bethany wondered whether she might have enjoyed it if she knew she was going to be saved. Two weeks previously, on one of their bucket list days, she had made Ebenezer take her on a rollercoaster, and she had loved it, even though he'd trembled for hours afterwards.

"Do it again," said Bethany. "This time, go higher."

The beast shrugged Claudette's wings and flew Bethany even further beyond the clouds, before dropping her again. This time, she screamed for joy.

They did this as they flew to the orphanage. Bethany was having fun, because she knew that Claudette would always be there to catch her, whilst the beast liked thinking that Bethany could smash into the ground at any moment.

In between the screams, they would peek and peer at the people below who were making their way to the theatre. Many of them were chatting excitedly about the evening that lay ahead of them. A day ago, Bethany would have loved to join in with their excited chatter, but now she just looked forward to destroying their happiness.

The beast landed Bethany on the opposite side from the orphanage. It started to fly away.

"Hey! Where are you going?" shouted Bethany.

"What are you looking for, a snack or something?" asked the beast. It lifted one of Claudette's talons in the air and farted out a stinky, greyish egg. When it cracked open, the street was filled with the stench of a gone-off shepherd's pie. " I need to set up a camera at the theatre because I'm broadcasting the performance for someone special. I'm sure you'll be able to bring Gloria in on your own."

The beast flew away, leaving Bethany unable to ask any questions about broadcasting or special guests. She crossed the road and pushed open the rusted orphanage gates.

Gloria was holding her final hijacking rehearsal on the front lawn. There was no stage but this didn't matter, because Gloria was happy to use Timothy's back instead. She scraped her tap-shoes down his spine as she shouted her feedback into the microphone.

"And when I sing the catapult song this time, I expect more applause!" barked Gloria at the children, whose hands were already red raw from over-clapping. She produced Bethany's catapult from the back of her costume and waved it around. "If you don't show more appreciation, then I'll be holding another motivational exercise!"

"Oh, please don't, Gloria," said Geoffrey, who had been forced to sit in the front row. "Poor Amy nearly lost an eye during the last game."

"Well then, what are you going to do about it?" asked Gloria, expectantly.

The children applauded Gloria once more, wincing with pain every time they brought their raw palms together. Gloria took deep, unnecessary bows, as if she had just delivered the performance of a lifetime. Bethany felt it was time to step in.

"Oi, Gloria! Are you coming or what?" she shouted.

Gloria interrupted her bow to turn her nose up at Bethany.

"Who dares to disturb the star at work?" asked Gloria.

"Me, obviously. Are you thick or something?" said Bethany.

Geoffrey stood up and smiled at Bethany. He started doing a double-handed, flappy wave, then decided against it, and returned his hands to the pockets of his theatre trousers.

"There we go, that's more like it!" said Gloria pointing at Geoffrey. "A standing, waving ovation is exactly what we want to see."

The exhausted children gave Geoffrey a loathsome stare, as they slowly got to their feet and started doing double-handed, flappy waves. Gloria took another deep bow.

"Actually, I was just saying hello to Bethany," mumbled Geoffrey.

Gloria dug her tap shoes into Timothy.

"Get it over with then," she said.

Geoffrey coughed and fiddled with his jumper, before saying, "Hello! What did you think of the latest issue of *D.I. Tortoise*?"

Bethany couldn't believe Geoffrey had the audacity to behave like this, when she knew full well that he hated her. She thought he might deserve three rats in the eye instead of two.

"I haven't read your stupid comic yet, so you can bog off," she said, causing Geoffrey to looked glumly at his jumper. "Come on Gloria, I've been sent to bring you to the theatre."

Gloria's eyes lit up. "The theatre?"

"Yeah, the Cussocks really want to see you," said Bethany.

Gloria's eyes lit up even brighter – so much so that they

appeared to be in danger of bursting into flames. "Do you mean I won't have to hijack anything this time? Do they really want to see *me*?"

Bethany experienced her first pang of guilt, just below the ribs, when she saw how delighted Gloria had been made by her lie. She tried to slap the pang away as she removed the silver rope from her backpack.

"Your parents asked me to tie this around your wrists," said Bethany. "I don't know why."

"It's experimental theatre, Bethany. I wouldn't expect you to understand," said Gloria, in her affected voice. She stepped down from Timothy. "Clearly I'm going to play a very important part in tonight's performance."

Bethany tried to tie a loose knot, but the rope had other ideas, and pulled itself tighter around Gloria's wrists. She unfolded the scooter from her backpack, and flicked it to its lowest setting, because she didn't want to deal with the inconvenience of Gloria falling into the road.

Whilst she was flying, Bethany had thought this moment would feel awesome, but instead she found herself feeling awkward, and the pangs of guilt grew stronger. As they zoomed out of the orphanage, she reminded herself that Gloria deserved everything that was coming to her.

The Hurtful Memories

Ebenezer had never disliked an item of clothing so much. There was a time in the eighteenth century when he experienced strong feelings of disregard for a certain style of hat that happened to be in fashion, but that was nothing compared to the hatred he felt for the gold-buttoned shirt.

The shirt made Ebenezer watch the television that the beast had hooked up to the memory book. Every time he tried to talk over the memories, the shirt would strangle him. Every time he tried to move his head away from the screen, the shirt would grow tighter around his chest, or turn itchy on his skin.

The book had run out of happy memories about the beast, so it was replaying ones it had already shown.

The book showed the beast doing its mildly amusing impression of Queen Victoria, and the help that it had given to ensure that Ebenezer was the most fabulously dressed man in the first age of jazz and jazzy trousers. There were clips of the beast vomiting out bomb-proof shutters to protect the house during wartime, and sparkly boom boxes to make sure that the house wouldn't be left out during disco-time. The book even showed up to the moment when the beast had vomited out the baby grand piano, just a few weeks ago.

When Ebenezer had first seen these same memories, just a couple of days ago, he had been secretly thrilled. Now the memories repulsed him. There's nothing like being kidnapped and tortured to make you go off someone.

All Ebenezer could think of was getting him and Bethany as far away from the beast as possible. His only chance of escape seemed to lie in the marks that Claudette's talons had left on the floor. The marks were words, and the words were:

THEY'RE YOUR MEMORIES. USE THEM.

At first, Ebenezer presumed that the message was just some cruel trick of the beast's, but the longer he looked at them, the more he thought it might have come from Claudette – or, at least, whatever was still left of her in the beast.

Ebenezer tried and tried to think about how he could possibly use his memories to escape, but he couldn't figure it out. He was terribly cross, because he knew he wouldn't be able to live with himself if he didn't find a way to save Bethany. There was nothing he had ever wanted more in the world than to see her again.

As Ebenezer thought about how much he missed Bethany, the portraits in the memory book began to change, and soon the TV was filled with clips of her. But because the beast was no longer the subject, the memories were unflattering ones.

The book showed Ebenezer picking up Bethany from the orphanage, when she had insulted his whistling, messed up his house and demanded to be fed nothing but chocolate cake. Then it showed how Bethany had used this chocolate cake to doodle over all his favourite paintings in the house. There were lots of clips of Bethany calling him charming names like 'nincompoop', 'nitwit' and 'gitface', and the book reminded him of his stroppy feelings whenever Bethany had tried to make him do something that got in the way of his easy life.

In spite of the book's efforts, Ebenezer took far more joy from seeing Bethany at her worst than he had from seeing the beast at its loathsome best. It was strange, but the clips of Bethany seemed to have an effect on the shirt and the other items as well. They squirmed and wriggled – deeply uncomfortable at the sight of Ebenezer and Bethany's friendship. It was like how the memory book and shirt had reacted when Ebenezer had tried doing do-gooding – none of the beastly items seemed to enjoy being in the vicinity of anything good or pure.

Ebenezer's eyes welled with tears when he looked at Bethany's face, but then the screen began to change again. He expected a transition to some new series of bad Bethany memories, but the beast appeared instead.

The beast was speaking live from a dressing room in the theatre, and it was looking straight down the lens of a camera it had put out for itself. Ebenezer saw that Claudette's beak was askew and that her body was battered and bruised. Feathers were falling from her body like petals from a dying rose.

"Excuse my appearance. It won't be this way for much longer," said the beast. "Soon, my usual glorious form will take over, but I'm staying parroty for as long as I can. It'll be such a nice touch to eat Bethany whilst still wearing the face of her only remaining friend, don't you think?"

Ebenezer wrestled against the shirt, and shouted in hoarse whispers.

"What was that?" asked the beast, as it leaned Claudette's ear to the camera. "Was it the sound of you begging for an exclusive backstage tour?"

The screen in the attic went wavy and wobbly, as the beast scooped up the camera in Claudette's wings and walked over to the stage. The beast panned the camera around, and showed that the baby grand piano was perched behind the curtain.

"I made it walk itself here from the bird-keeper's," said the beast. "I think it'll really add some pizazz to the evening."

The beast walked further up the stage. Ebenezer heard the excited hustle and bustle of a live audience, and then he saw their faces when the beast poked the camera between the curtains.

It seemed like everyone in the neighbourhood was crammed into the creaky confines of the Cussock Theatre.

Eduardo and his fellow Barnacles were sat in the front row, and he was wearing a fancy new shirt, bought with Ebenezer's money. The lizard lady and Jared Kettlefletch were seated together a few rows behind, and the Cussocks themselves were a few rows back from that. The bird-keeper was in the upper tier with Keith the Dove on his lap, negotiating with Miss Muddle about the price of her merry malty-nuts.

"Look at them all," said the beast. "They've come here for an unforgettable night at the theatre, and by goodness we're going to give it to them. Just as soon as Bethany brings Gloria through those doors . . ."

Ebenezer shouted and wrestled against the shirt again.

"Shh, shh – don't worry, I know you're impatient for the show to start as well," said the beast, smirking through Claudette's wonky beak. "I promise that I'll link you back in the very moment it begins."

The beast blew a kiss through Claudette's beak. Then it switched off the camera.

The television in the attic went blank. A few moments later, it flickered back to life with more images from the memory book. The latest ones were clips of Bethany shouting at Ebenezer in the aftermath of the apology party.

Ebenezer looked at the message that Claudette had left again:

THEY'RE YOUR MEMORIES. USE THEM.

An idea popped into his head. He closed his eyes, and focused on his real memories of Bethany – the ones that showed their true friendship.

He thought about the first bucket-list day they had spent together, when they insulted the staff at Buckingham Palace. He thought about the time a few days ago, when they had laughed with each other after mistaking do-gooding for drinking soup and doing laundry, and he thought about the times she had laid out his favourite comic, or tried showing him the correct approach to buttering bread or folding napkins. He remembered the last good moment they'd had together, when he'd told her about his accidental spot of do-gooding, and she had looked at him with such pride and surprise.

Ebenezer opened his eyes and saw that the look on her face was on the television now. Soon afterwards, all the other memories he had relived started flickering on the screen.

The beastly things hadn't liked seeing the bad times of Ebenezer and Bethany's friendship, but they positively hated seeing the good times.

The shirt loosened around Ebenezer's body, as if physically allergic to the television. Ebenezer wriggled with all his might and ripped it from his chest, sending gold buttons scattering across the floor.

The other items reacted in the same way. The memory book burst into blue flames, and the flames were caught by the self-decorating Christmas tree, which whirred its branches around its trunk like an out-of-control chainsaw. The tree in turn set fire to the other objects – causing Raphael the rubber ducky to melt, and the astronaut suit to fade away like a dying star. Even the television itself cracked, as if it could no longer bear to project such images.

The attic was ablaze with blue flames, but then the fire died as quickly as it started – with nothing from the real world being set alight by the burning of the beastly objects. It was like they somehow no longer had an effect on actual things.

Ebenezer never thought he'd be so happy to bid farewell to the beast's gifts. He dashed across the room and slammed the attic door behind him. He sprinted across floors and slid down bannisters. When he got to the ground floor, he was surprised to hear the doorbell ring.

He hoped to find Bethany standing on the other side of it, but instead he found Mr Clinke. The old man was wearing a battered red suit, and he had given his walking sticks a polish. Nurse Mindy was waiting in her car at the end of the drive.

"You look terrible," said the old man.

"I feel far from dandy," croaked Ebenezer.

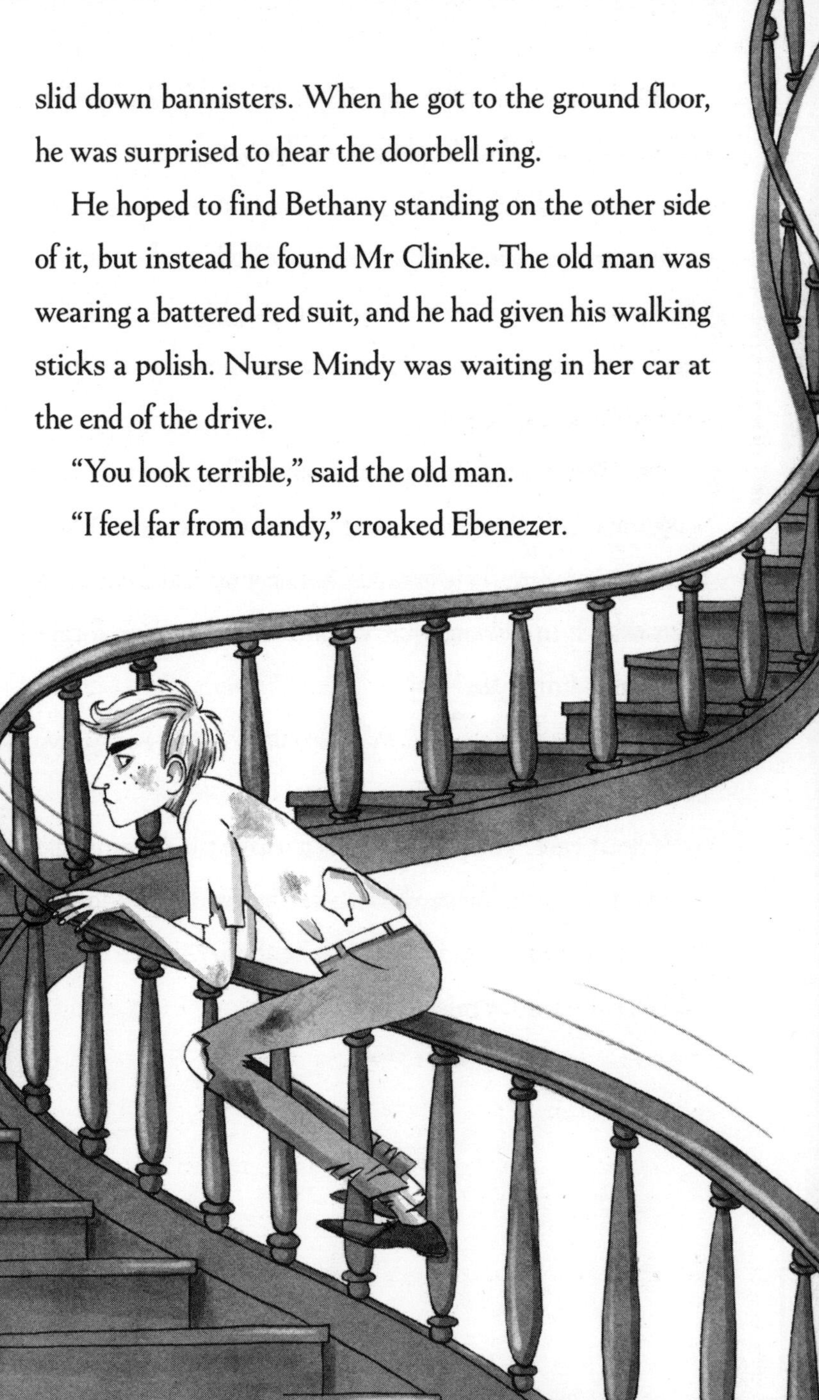

"Here, have one of these." The old man rummaged in his pockets, until he found a box of cough sweets.

Ebenezer didn't think that a cough sweet was going to do much to counteract a solid day of strangulation, but after a few sucks his throat felt thoroughly soothed. He was able to speak at a normal volume again, and the bruises around his neck began to fade.

"Are these magical sweets?" asked Ebenezer.

"Don't be ridiculous. They're scientific sweets. Dorris made them for me." He looked Ebenezer up and down, and then asked, in a somewhat wounded voice, "You forgot about me, didn't you?"

"No, no, of course not. Well, actually, yes – sorry, I've been a bit tied up," said Ebenezer.

"I don't care. You promised me a trip to the theatre, and I've been looking forward to it all day," said the old man. "Chuck on a shirt and join me when you're quite ready. I'll be cranky if we miss the start."

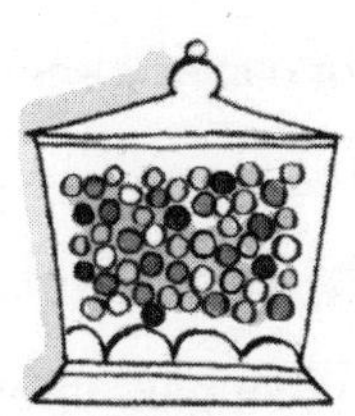

The Pre-Show Nerves

"Will you please loosen this rope?" asked Gloria. "Acting is impossible without the use of extravagant hand gestures!"

They were about five minutes from the theatre. Bethany was still scootering at the slowest speed, which meant that several cars overtook them. They were even overtaken by the orphanage bus, filled with Timothy and the other children.

Usually, Gloria would have kicked up a big fuss about such a thing, but she was in a dreamy mood because of what Bethany had told her.

"Did Mummy and Daddy really say they wanted to see me?" asked Gloria, as they continued to zoom towards the theatre. "What words did they use?"

"One of them said they wanted to see you, and the other said yeah OK," said Bethany.

"*Yeah OK* . . . what a nice thing for them to say," said Gloria, with a sigh. "What about their faces? How did they look when they said they wanted to see me?"

"I dunno. They looked like normal people saying normal things," said Bethany, who was still struggling with the pangs of guilt. "Stop asking stupid questions about it."

"Don't take that tone with me. Need I remind you that I am the talent, and you are the driver?" said Gloria. "There's no need to be bitter just because your parents died in a fire."

"I'd rather have dead parents who loved me than alive ones who don't care," said Bethany.

She immediately regretted saying this, because sometimes it's better to lose an argument than win it. Bethany wished that Gloria would respond with something even nastier, but all she received in return was silence.

"You deserved that," said Bethany. She tried to look at Gloria's eyes, but her face was turned away.

"I deserve nothing but standing ovations and bouquets of flowers from my adoring fans!" cried Gloria.

"Nah. You deserve a lot worse," said Bethany. She was trying to convince herself that she was still doing the right thing. "If you were nicer to the people at the orphanage, maybe you'd have more adoring fans."

"What are you talking about? The other children love me!" said Gloria.

"Yeah, about as much as your parents love you," said Bethany.

Once again, Bethany felt rotten with regret. Being cruel to one's enemies is like chopping off your arm just so you can hit them with it – in the end, all you do is cause more damage to yourself.

"I had no idea you were so unpleasant," said Gloria.

"Actually, up until recently, I was trying to become a better person," said Bethany.

"It's not working," said Gloria. "And what do you mean the children don't like me? I'm wonderfully generous with my time. There aren't many stars who would let their audience play such an important role in their careers."

"You chase them around the orphanage with a catapult," said Bethany.

"That's method acting!"

"You make them carry you around the place on a throne."

"I'm involving them in my artistic process!"

"They've all injured their hands clapping and preparing your ridiculous costumes."

"It's not my fault they haven't learned to sew or applaud, and I would say they are receiving valuable skills for life."

Bethany wondered whether it was possible that Gloria didn't know how much everyone hated her. Bethany began to pity her, but then she remembered why she was driving her to the theatre in the first place.

"My apology party . . . you stopped everyone from coming," said Bethany.

"What party?" asked Gloria.

"Don't try that trick on me," said Bethany.

"I'm not trying anything on you," said Gloria. "I never get invited to parties. I think it's because people think I'm too much of a big star to come. Whereas the truth is that I would happily attend as many as possible, because the crowds that gather there offer me a perfect chance to practise my song and dance numbers."

Bethany turned her head. Gloria was a terrible actress, which meant Bethany should have been able to tell when she was lying, however, she seemed deadly serious.

"Nah," said Bethany. "You know exactly what I'm talking about. Next, you'll be trying to claim that you didn't beat up Claudette."

"Beat up Claudette? I would never beat anyone up – even

theatre critics," said Gloria. "I wouldn't dare risk injuring my beautiful hands. Like I said, hand gestures are terribly important to my process."

Bethany glanced behind her again, just as they were approaching the theatre. She looked at Gloria's hands and saw that there was no evidence of any cuts or bruises that would have certainly been there if she had punched Claudette in the beak.

"Hand gestures will be particularly important for this catapult song I've got planned," said Gloria. "Do you want to hear how it goes?"

Bethany gripped the scooter's handlebars tighter, as she tried to figure out what it all meant. Gloria was clearly telling the truth, but that couldn't be possible, because it meant Claudette had been lying to her the whole time.

"Of course you do. Well, here goes. Imagine that you're watching me dance a beautiful tap dance whilst I sing the chorus," said Gloria. "*Cats go miaow, my catapult makes you say oww. If a cat were hit by my catapult, it would say miaowowowww* . . . I'm hoping the audience will join in on the 'miaowowoww' bit. Do you like it?"

"I don't like one bit about this," said Bethany.

She tried turning the scooter away from the theatre, but

the scooter had other ideas. It kept its wheels pointed at the theatre, and dialled itself up to the quickest speed setting.

"This is more like it!" shouted Gloria. She shouted some more, but Bethany couldn't hear a word because they were whizzing through the air so fast.

The scooter didn't slow itself until they were inside the lobby of the Cussock Theatre – right next to Miss Muddle's sweet stand. Gloria hopped off the scooter, took a deep bow, and informed Miss Muddle that she would be willing to sign autographs after the show, once her hands were untied.

"You?!" said Miss Muddle. But much to Gloria's irritation, she was addressing Bethany. "I can't believe you have the cheek to come here!"

"Soz, Miss Muddle, but I've got no time to—" began Bethany.

"Yes, I should think that you are 'soz'. You and your parrot," said Miss Muddle. "I'll be fishing frogs and purple feathers out of my sweet shop for weeks!"

"Purple feathers? In your sweet shop?" asked Bethany. She felt like her world was crashing around her.

"Well, this is all very fascinating, but I've got a show to perform," said Gloria. "Now if you'd excuse – graaggghhhh!"

Gloria graaggghhhhed because the silver rope started dragging her through the aisle that led to the stage. Bethany ran after her, with a puzzled Miss Muddle following behind.

The audience naturally thought that this strange behaviour marked the beginning of the show. The lights were dimmed by the Cussocks, and everyone started applauding and whooping with great enthusiasm.

Gloria was dragged by the silver rope until she was right in front of the stage. She was turned around to face the green velvet curtain.

After the audience's whoops and cheers died down,

the curtain slowly opened. The stage floor was filled with enough feathers to fill a pillow factory. In front of the piano, there stood a grotesque half-parrot, half-beastly creature.

Instead of feet, it had talons. And instead of a mouth, it had half a beak. One half of its body was feathered, whilst the other was grey and blobby.

"Good evening, ladies and gentlemen. Welcome to my show!" said the beast. "I do hope you're all sitting comfortably. You're in for quite the performance."

"Oh no, Claudette . . ." said Bethany.

The Theatre of Screams

The beast hopped onto the baby-grand piano, and vomited out an old-fashioned microphone. The audience whooped and cheered again, thinking that it was all part of the concert. Geoffrey even gave a standing ovation, because he happened to be a great fan of magic.

The piano played a little light jazz, whilst the beast spoke with soft, slithery tones into the microphone.

"Ladies and gentlemen, there has been a slight change to the very soul of this show," said the beast. The wing on the parroty side of its body fell off, and a tiny, beastly arm began to grow. "I know all the posters for this evening have promised it would be a *Patrick Extravaganza*, but I've decided to use the evening to focus on someone else

entirely. Ladies and gentlemen, please welcome the one and only Bethany to the theatre!"

The beast pointed its new beastly arm into the aisle, causing the theatre spotlights to shine their bright, hot light into Bethany's eyes. The audience clapped and whooped again, in spite of the fact that none of them cared all that much for her at the moment.

Bethany raised her hand to her face – partly to block the spotlight, but mainly because she couldn't bear to look at the sight of Claudette being beastified. Claudette had been the best parrot and the wisest person she had ever known. More importantly, she had been one of her only three friends – and she couldn't believe that she hadn't seen the signs of her transformation.

"Thank you for your enthusiasm, ladies and gentlemen, but in your excitement I fear you're making the wrong sort of noises," said the beast, with a sad shake of its half-feathered, half-blobby head. "Claps and cheers are not the sort of things that should be given to a girl like Bethany. Once you've seen what's she's brought with her, I'm sure you'll agree that some boos and hisses would suit her far better. Unzip your backpack for the lovely people to see, Bethany."

Bethany felt the eyes of the entire theatre upon her. Soon the whole theatre was chanting at her to reveal the contents of her backpack. Even Geoffrey got involved, because he presumed Bethany was in on whatever joke the beast was playing.

"There's no escaping it, Bethany. You might as well reveal the truth about yourself now, or I'll just have to come down and do it myself," said the beast.

Bethany didn't feel like Bethany as she shrugged off her backpack. The shock and devastation of the beastly truth made her feel like some hollowed-out shell – more of a puppet than a person.

As the rats and the nose-pegs tumbled out, she saw the last few days afresh, through the lens of the beast's plan. She saw how everything had been staged – the apology party, the frogs in Miss Muddle's sweet shop, the surprisingly helpful behaviour of the beastly items, the Gloria 'big shock', and even *The Patrick Extravaganza* itself – all designed to lead up to this moment.

"Some of you in this audience might have heard that she has given up her bad ways, but I am here to tell you that this is not the case," said the beast. "Do you see those rats? She brought them here today to superstinkbomb each and every one of you!"

Jared Kettlefletch stood up from his seat, and spat through his gold teeth.

"It's true!" he said. "She bought them from . . . *some* shop I know about . . . I can't believe she was going to use them against me!"

"How fascinating," said the beast, positively purring with delight. "Tell me, can anyone see anything else of interest that tumbled out of Bethany's backpack?"

Everyone in the theatre turned to look at the things strewn across the aisle, but Miss Muddle was the first to spot what the beast was talking about. She bent down and picked up the torn page of health inspector numbers.

"Now then, Bethany, what could you possibly want with those numbers?" asked the beast.

"After the show, I was gonna take the rats to the sweet shop," said Bethany. She spoke blankly, as if reading from a dull Geography textbook. She knew when she was beaten. "I was gonna call the health inspector, so they'd see the rats in the shop before Miss Muddle could do anything about it."

"Bethany! I could have lost my sweet shop!" said Miss Muddle.

"I didn't think of that," said Bethany. She looked down to her shoes, because she couldn't stand to meet anyone's eyes after all the bad she had done. "I just wanted you to know what it's like to be blamed for something that's not your fault."

The audience were now fully on board with the beast's booing and hissing proposal. And as they booed, more audience members stood up to confirm Bethany's villainy.

"She tried to volunteer in my shop!" said the bird-keeper, causing Keith the Dove to coo a boo in agreement. "She probably had summat similarly nasty planned for me too!"

"She and her friend sold me a shirt that tried to kill me!" shouted Eduardo Barnacle.

"She sent Gloria Cussock up to catapult me!" said Timothy.

"There is a LOT of elephant poop missing from my zoo!" croaked the lizard lady, causing some confusion in the audience, because she had failed to provide any context to this comment.

The beast opened Claudette's beak wide, and breathed in all the hatred that was pouring out on Bethany, feeling strengthened by every horrid comment. It adored having the audience in the palms of its tiny hands.

"These pranks only show one part of her terrible nature," said the beast. "And what I'm about to tell you now will shock you to your core."

It wiggled its fingers and used the silver rope to drag Gloria up on to the stage.

"Bethany hates this girl. In fact, she hates this girl so much that she suggested I should eat her as a showtime snack," said the beast, causing gasps aplenty to burst from the audience. Gloria's bottom lip wobbled as she realised that her parents had never really wanted to see her at all. "Naturally, I said I wouldn't dream of doing such a thing. But Bethany wouldn't listen and has brought her to me anyway. She even tried beating me up, so I would do it for her."

"NO – it's not true! I didn't . . ." began Bethany. The sentence died in her mouth, because she knew nothing she said would make any difference.

The Cussocks stood up from their seats at the back of the theatre.

"Please don't eat our daughter!" said Mr Cussock.

"Yes, it would completely damage the reputation of our theatre!" said Mrs Cussock.

They sat back down again, feeling that they had done all they were prepared to do. The beast wiggled its fingers and dragged Gloria closer to its mouth, whilst she screamed and resisted against the silver rope.

"Ladies and gentlemen, I'm not sure about you, but I think that Bethany deserves some sort of punishment for her actions . . ."

The audience roared in agreement.

"She needs to learn that you can't hurt the people of this neighbourhood and get away with it . . ."

The audience roared louder. Keith the Dove cooed like he had never cooed before.

"... and that's why, ladies and gentlemen, I'm going to eat her alive, on this very stage – tonight!"

The beast spread out its tiny hands, and prepared to bathe in the thunder of righteous applause. However, the audience ceased roaring and cooing immediately. The beast presumed they hadn't heard its wonderful suggestion.

"I said, I'M GOING TO EAT HER ALIVE!" it boomed again.

The theatre remained quieter than an abandoned library. Many mouths dropped open in horror.

"Oh, come on, don't go soft on me now," said the beast. It hated feeling the audience slipping away from its grasp. "We all know that she deserves it."

Bethany stepped forward. She seemed to be the only person in the theatre still capable of speech.

"Yeah. I definitely do," she said. "I won't put up a fight, if you let everyone else here go."

Bethany walked towards the stage. The parroty side of the beast's body started to twitch in the face of such selflessness.

"No – don't do that. Don't you dare try and make this

some kind of do-gooding act," said the beast, twitching more as Bethany walked closer and closer up the aisle. "You're evil! You're just like me – I've just proved it!"

The audience began to murmur amongst themselves. Bethany could be a menace, but even the lizard lady questioned whether she deserved to be eaten alive.

"Oh, bother, please stop it!" said Geoffrey, standing up. "Bethany shouldn't be—"

The piano abruptly stopped playing, and the beast snarled through the remains of Claudette's beak. It vomited out a large yellow umbrella, and sent it flying above Geoffrey's head.

"People who talk at the theatre deserve to be puddled," said the beast.

The umbrella opened above Geoffrey's head, sucked up his wriggling body, and closed itself again. A few moments later, it spat out a puddle through its handle.

"NO!" shouted Bethany. She ran over to the puddle, and cried because the second of her three only friends in the world had been killed by the beast. She felt like it was all her fault.

The theatre was filled with screams, as the beast's big yellow brolly flew around the theatre. "SHUT UP!" the beast bellowed. "Anyone who tries to leave *will* be puddled."

The audience sat in their seats, thoroughly terrified. They didn't quite shut up, but they managed to dial down their screams to some murmured wailing and stifled sobbing.

"Now then, I am going to eat Bethany – and each and every one of you will cheer me on!"

The beast wiggled its fingers – causing the rope to slither off Gloria's hands and wrap itself around Bethany's instead. It dragged her up on to the stage, whilst she wriggled with all her might.

"I said CHEER!" said the beast.

The audience cheered feebly, even though they were feeling distinctly uncheery. The beast dragged Bethany closer to its mouth. It wrapped its two black tongues around Claudette's beak and snapped it off, so that it would be able to eat her better.

"Ladies and gentlemen, I'm only going to ask you this question once, and if you care about your life, you're going to shout your answer as loudly as possible," said the beast. It turned Bethany around so she would hear the audience calling out for her death. "SHOULD I EAT BETHANY ALIVE NOW?"

"NO!" shouted a lone voice at the back of the

theatre, quicker than anyone else could speak.

The owner of the voice stepped into the spotlight. He was an incredibly old, yet impossibly young man, wearing a hastily thrown-on pyjama top, paired with some exquisite trousers.

"NO!" said Ebenezer Tweezer again. "This stops – right now. I won't let you hurt anyone else."

The Puddling

"Who's a clever boy then?" said the beast, doing its best parrot voice. "Did you really manage to break out of the attic all by yourself? I'm terribly impressed."

Ebenezer's voice had been soothed, but the rest of his body was still battered and bruised. As Bethany looked at him, she realised that Ebenezer had never abandoned her – and that it was all another part of the beast's dreadful scheme.

"Run Ebenezer, it's too late!" she shouted. She couldn't bear to see her third, final, and most important friend killed by the beast.

"Don't you dare send my dear boy away," said the beast. "Look at him – he's positively desperate to see his beasty in action. I think he deserves a premier seat."

The beast wiggled its fingers and brought the big yellow brolly hovering over the best seat in the house – which happened to be occupied by Eduardo Barnacle. The beast puddled Eduardo right in between his screaming parents.

"There you go, Ebenezer. Would you like me to vomit out a blanket so your bottom doesn't get wet?" said the beast.

"Stop it – stop it right now!" said Ebenezer, marching up the aisle.

"Oh deary. First you break out of the attic, and now you think you're some kind of hero, do you? It seems like someone's been reading too many comics," said the beast, with a sad shake of its head. "I must say I'm rather fascinated to see what you have in mind. Is that man with the walking sticks a part of your plan?"

The beast looked behind Ebenezer. The old man was slowly hobbling into the theatre, even though Ebenezer had given him explicit instructions to go back to the retirement home with Nurse Mindy.

"I haven't come here with a plan. I've come here to offer you a deal," said Ebenezer. "Let's run away from here. You and I – let's go right now."

"What?" said the beast. A smirk broke out across its dribbly lips – causing more feathers to fall from the parroty side of its body. "You want me to throw away all this hard work? Why on earth would I do that?"

"Because I'll serve you again."

"You'll serve me again whether you like it or not."

"No, I mean I'll do it willingly – like the days before the Bethany blip," said Ebenezer. "I know you can get me to do whatever you like either way, by beating and bullying, but wouldn't you rather avoid all that fuss? If you let her go, I promise I will be the best servant you've ever had. I'll bring you your meals, and I won't ask for anything in return. Staff like that is hard to find. It's like you said – everyone else who served you proved too weak and widdly, m-master."

The smirk grew wider. The beast liked hearing the word 'master' again.

"No, Ebenezer! I'll never let the beast be the boss of you again!" said Bethany.

"You don't have a choice in the matter. Please be quiet whilst I speak with my master," said Ebenezer. He returned his attention to the beast. "Think about it. You can't stay here – this show will have attracted too much attention —"

"Don't worry about these people, I was planning

on puddling them all anyway," said the beast.

This remark did not go down well with the audience.

"That seems like a lot of hassle for you," said Ebenezer. "It would be so much easier if we were to leave right now. We could be far away – long before any division even comes near here. It could be a fresh start – wouldn't that be good for us?"

"I suppose an attic in a slightly hotter country could be interesting," said the beast. "But I'm not getting it – you wouldn't want anything from me? No new tea sets, no trousers jazzy enough to play the saxophone? What about the magical things you used to demand from me?"

"I don't need any of that," said Ebenezer. "Just let Bethany live, and I'll serve you until the end of time."

He looked at Bethany, and Bethany looked at him. They had only known each other for a short time, but their friendship was the most important thing to have happened in Ebenezer's long, long life. If this was the last time that he was going to see Bethany, he needed her to know how much she meant to him.

"You see, master. A change of scene would be good, because I'm turning a bit weak and widdly myself," said Ebenezer, choosing his words carefully. "For some reason, I've grown attached to this peculiar prankster. She's bossy, she never says 'thank you', she has the table manners of a warthog, and . . . as you've so cleverly shown, master . . . she's got a long way to go before she's anywhere near being a good person. But, deep down, she wants to be better – and there's something rather wonderful about that."

The beast was so busy smiling about the 'clever' compliment that it failed to take in what Ebenezer was actually saying. The audience all listened closely – willing Ebenezer not to do anything stupid.

"When we thought you were gone, master, Bethany could have done anything. She could have lived every day as a bucket-list day – using my money to do just about anything in the world – or she could have just slobbed about reading comics and watching TV all the time," said Ebenezer. "It's what I would have done, and no one would have blamed her for doing it – especially given how hard her life has been. And yet, she tried to make up for the menace she caused by being a do-gooder instead."

A few members of the audience shifted in their seats, with the bird-keeper and Keith the Dove feeling particularly bad for the things they had said and cooed. Meanwhile, the parroty side of the beast's body started to twitch ever so lightly.

"Yes, she fell down by plotting revenge, but we all fall down from time to time, don't we? And, when it came down to it, I'm not sure if Bethany would have actually been able to go through with the pranks she had planned, because it's much easier imagining mean things, rather than actually doing them," said Ebenezer. "The most important thing is that she wants to be better. And she wants to help other people be better too – even selfish gitfaces like me, master."

Bethany blushed, until she was almost as purple as the feathers that were falling from the beast's body. For some stupid reason, her eyes had decided to water as well.

"Stop it, Ebenezer," said the beast. It's twitching grew more pronounced, and, as it did so, the big yellow brolly wobbled and the rope around Bethany's wrists began to loosen.

"That's what I'm saying master," said Ebenezer. "We've got to stop me from spending any more time with her, because she's making me far too weak and widdly. The thought of not seeing her again makes me want to cry, because I'll miss everything about her. Heck, I think I might even miss her sandwiches. So, that's why we need to move far away from here, master."

"I know what you're doing," said the beast. Its voice was uneven, because its parroty side was now trembling uncontrollably. "It won't work, there's hardly anything left of her. I mean NOTHING, there's NOTHING left of her."

"What's it on about?" asked Bethany.

"Claudette," said Ebenezer. He spoke quickly now, no longer using the soft tones he'd used to address the beast. "If we can find some way of helping her take back her body, then maybe —"

"There is no way of helping her, Ebenezer! You're going to need more than a pretty speech to bring her back," said the beast.

It turned its twitching body towards Bethany, wiggled its fingers and opened its mouth. All it got was a mouthful of its own vomit, because Bethany had wriggled out of the rope's grasp.

"Something more than a speech," Bethany said to herself, as she thought of what could possibly be powerful enough to get through to Claudette. She grimaced when she realised what she had to do. "Oh no. I am *not* a singer."

"Eh?" said Ebenezer. He jumped on the stage, and stepped in front of Bethany to guard her from the beast.

"I'm talking about Claudette's flipping favourite song. The one that always makes her think that she can do anything in the world," she said. Then, very reluctantly,

she sang; "*The hurricane's here, oh but not for us . . .*"

Ebenezer remembered what the beast said about what good songs did to the soul. He joined Bethany in the next line.

"*When I have you near, oh there is no fuss,*" they sang, whilst Ebenezer waved his arms for others to join in.

The remaining Barnacles were the first to stand up, because they were desperate to do anything that could avenge the killer of their son. Gloria Cussock was the next – and she bellowed in a loud voice from the stage. The bird-keeper and Keith the Dove joined half-way through the next line.

"*Let's dance a waltz love, and sing to our song . . .*"

The beast spat out the silver rope and sent it chasing Bethany around the theatre. The beast also threatened to puddle anyone who dared sing a single word of the song, but this didn't stop more voices joining in, when the people saw the effect that it was having.

"*Lay out the best mat, click the kettle on . . .*"

Soon, even the most reluctant audience members, like the lizard lady and Jared Kettlefletch, added their voices to the choir – partly to save Bethany, but mainly to save themselves from a creature who seemed so relaxed about puddling people to death.

The song, so dear to Claudette, in combination with the fact that the audience was risking death to sing it, proved unbearable for the beast.

"Nothing can hurt us, 'cause we're together . . ."

The beast's arms shrivelled into its blobby flesh, and the flesh itself sprouted new feathers, wings, and a beak for the mouth. The piano tried to play a loud, unmelodic tune to block out the melody's power, but one instrument was no match for an entire theatre of people singing for their life.

"Let this hurricane go on forever!"

By the time everyone started singing the chorus again, Claudette was back in the room. Her chest grew bigger, her eyes changed from shiny black to sparkling blue, and the general look of true kindness returned to her face. But, she wasn't finished there.

The beast had used Claudette's talents, and now it was time for her to repay the favour. With a single wiggle of her talons, she crumpled the piano into a ball and shrank the yellow brolly into something that could have fit inside a teeny, tiny cocktail. She raised her wings and de-puddled Geoffrey and Eduardo – causing them both to spring back to life, thoroughly confused about what had happened in

the time since they were puddled by the brolly.

Meanwhile, the old man was fiddling with the rats that Bethany had left in the aisle – replacing the stinkpods with something from his pockets. He seemed remarkably unaffected by the events that were taking place, and no one bothered to pay attention to him, because they were all focused on Claudette.

Bethany climbed back on to the stage, and tried to reach out to her friend. "No, Bethany – stay back!" said Claudette. "The beast is still here – trying to take back control. I need to find some way of getting it out!"

"Eggs!" said Ebenezer. "In the attic, the beast said you can get rid of it by pushing it out through an egg!"

Claudette nodded, and then her face contorted into a portrait of misery, as she shook her bottom and started laying the most painful egg of her life – one which contained something far more disgusting than any stale cake, runny sausage, or shepherd's pie. The purple on her face grew paler.

"Bethany, I . . . I just want to say . . . I'm sorry."

And with that, Claudette collapsed on the stage – just like she had done in the rehearsal. Only this time, a large, shiny blue egg rolled out of her bottom.

"Get back!" said Bethany, now standing in front of

Ebenezer to protect him.

"I may be able to help with that, Squeezer," said the old man, who had finally finished his business with the rats. He walked up the aisle quicker than Ebenezer had ever seen him move.

"Keep away, Mr Clinke," said Ebenezer. "Trust me – we don't want you to be anywhere near when that egg hatches."

"On the contrary, Squeezer. I think you'll want me to be as close to the egg as possible, so I can help you with it," said the old man. "Perhaps I should be clearer. I'm here as a representative of D.o.R.R.i.S. – the **D**ivision **o**f **R**emoving **R**apscallions **i**n **S**ecret. I believe you might have dealt with us in the past?"

The Man from DoRRiS

"W-W-What?" said Ebenezer. "No, you can't be, Mr Clinke!"

"I can be and I am. But I'm afraid my name isn't Clinke. I like to jumble up the letters of my name when I'm creating a new identity. The name's Nickle. Well, Mr Nicholas Nickle the Twenty-third if you want to be accurate about it," said the old man. "Do you remember my great-grandfather? The whole reason I joined D.o.R.R.i.S. in the first place was because of a story passed down in my family – one of an evil beast who threatened to puddle people, and a strange child named Loser."

"Ebenoozer Loser is not my name," said Ebenezer,

with as much dignity as he could muster.

"Is anyone gonna explain what the flip is going on?" asked Bethany.

"This is the retirement-home man I was telling you about," said Ebenezer. "The one who I thought I was helping."

"You *were* helping me," said Mr Nickle the Twenty-third. "But perhaps not in the way that you expected . . ."

Mr Nickle explained how one of the global D.o.R.R.i.S. knowledge gatherers flagged the beastly yard sale, and conducted a sweep for supernatural activity. After the sweep came back with intriguing results, D.o.R.R.i.S. decided to send their head agent and number one beast expert into the field.

"I arrived the day after the sale. I wanted to stay in a hotel, but D.o.R.R.i.S. insisted that I would blend in more at the retirement home," said Mr Nickle. "I headed straight for the house to inspect the items from the sale, and that's when you invited me in, Squeezer. As I was leaving, I planted a long-range listening device, so I would be able to hear everything that was going on."

Mr Nickle produced the formerly waxy hearing aid from his pocket. The audience would have oohed and ahhed if they had a clue what the hell was happening.

"Of course, my suspicions were on this Claudette character from the beginning, but every time I scanned her, the results just suggested that she was an incredibly healthy parrot," continued Mr Nickle. "So I bid my time and continued looking for clues. Those words you played during Word Jumble helped me an awful lot, Squeezer."

At the mention of Claudette's name, Bethany ran across the stage to check on her friend. She was unconscious, but she was breathing. On the other side of the stage, next to an increasingly perplexed Gloria, the beastly egg began to crack.

"In my time at D.o.R.R.i.S., I've captured werewolves, humanoids, vengeful ghosts, psychopathic printers, demonic iguanas, and even the great slug of the Black Sea. But nothing compares to this – after all, the beast was the whole reason why the organisation was set up in the first place," said Mr Nickle. "I don't know what I'll do next . . ."

The cracks spread across the egg like a spider stretching its legs. A few of the audience members who were seasoned pantomimegoers were quite tempted to shout out 'IT'S BEHIND YOU!', but sheer terror prevented them from opening their mouths.

"What happens to me?" asked Ebenezer, nervously.

"What do you mean?" asked Mr Nickle.

"I mean my beastly behaviour. All that time I kept it hidden," said Ebenezer.

"Oh, I see," said Mr Nickle. He scrunched up his wrinkly brow creating even more lines in his forehead. "Well, I think that your punishment for hiding the beast for five hundred years will have to be . . . well . . . the fact that you've lived with the beast for five hundred years. In my books, that's plenty of time served for bad behaviour."

Ebenezer was so exhausted from the sleeplessness in the attic that he nearly collapsed into sobs of relief, however he managed to pull himself together, because he didn't want to look stupid in front of his very first secret agent.

Whilst he was pulling himself together, a tiny, beastly hand pushed out of the egg. A few seconds later, the other did the same.

"I just can't believe I didn't realise you were a secret agent," said Ebenezer. "Then again, I suppose I probably only think of them wearing some cunning disguise."

"Who says I'm not wearing one?" said Mr Nickle.

"So you're not really that old and wrinkly?" asked Bethany.

"No, this is my real face. And I don't think I'm that wrinkly, thank you very much," said Mr Nickle. "However, I only need one walking stick."

Mr Nickle reached on to the stage and tapped the egg with one of his walking sticks, just as the beast's blobby head broke through the shell. The beast looked confused, disoriented, and completely unlike itself, as its whole body disappeared into the stick.

The audience burst into a round of applause. Geoffrey even gave a standing ovation, because he happened to be a great fan of weaponised walking sticks.

"Where did the beast go?" asked Ebenezer.

"Into the stick. Obviously. I'm awfully dangerous with D.o.R.R.i.S. sticks like these," said Mr Nickle. "There's a mobile prison unit inside that was strong enough to contain the world-destroying giantess of Mars, so it should do the trick. Also, it's useful if my legs get tired and I do need two sticks after all."

The D.o.R.R.i.S. stick began to shake in Mr Nickle's hand.

"Hmm, haven't seen that before," said Mr Nickle. "Should probably get this back to base as soon as possible. But first . . . "

Mr Nickle climbed onto the stage, demonstrating a surprising nimbleness. He walked over to Claudette, and told Bethany to stand to one side.

"There's also a life-support unit inside this stick. We sometimes have to use it to save the wounded on our intergalactic battlefields," said Mr Nickle. He fiddled with the settings on the top of the walking stick, and sucked Claudette inside. "It's the safest place for her until I get her back to base."

Worry was etched across Bethany's face. "Will she be OK?" she asked.

"I see no reason why she shouldn't be," said Mr Nickle. "Now, just one more thing . . ."

He rummaged around the used tissues in his pockets until he found the four nose-pegs he had picked up off the floor. He put one around his own nostrils, and gave the other three to Bethany, Ebenezer and Gloria.

"I hope you don't mind, Bethany, but I've replaced the odours you made with a little spray we D.o.R.R.i.S. agents use whenever missions attract a little too much attention. Those rats are most useful – saves me from having to spray everyone individually," said Mr Nickle, before he turned his attention to the audience. "Ladies and gentlemen, if I could have your attention for just one minute . . . "

Mr Nickle fiddled with the top of his stick whilst all eyes in the room were on him. Within a few moments, the red eyes of the rats came to life, and the creatures started scrabbling around the theatre – filling the place with a pink smoke that sent every member of the audience into a snore-filled slumber. He instructed the others when it was safe to remove their nose-pegs.

"I've altered their memories. When they wake up in about . . . oh, thirty seconds or so . . . they will believe that everything they've seen tonight was all a planned part of the show," he explained. "There's no reason why they should be burdened with knowledge of the beast."

"You what?" said Gloria. "But I was nearly eaten alive! I'm going to tell everyone about this – all the TV channels and news reporters. This is going to make me a star!"

"Without anyone to support your story, you're going to find it difficult to convince people you're telling the truth," said Mr Nickle. "Besides, now you have the chance to have starred in one of the tensest, most immersive shows that the Cussock Theatre has ever seen."

A few seconds later, true to Mr Nickle's prediction, the audience woke up. They all rose to their feet and offered a thunderous standing ovation for the apparently wonderful performance.

"Much better than a vat of elephant excrement!" croaked the lizard lady, who did not normally bestow such high praise on anything.

"Such wonderful special effects! We thought our boy had actually been puddled!" said Eduardo's parents.

"So many delightfully nasty twists and turns!" said Jared Kettlefletch, with a gold-toothed grin.

"Well worth every bleedin' penny!" said the bird-keeper, and Keith the Dove cooed in agreement.

Gloria looked into the crowd of adoring faces, and saw the adoration that she had wanted to receive for her entire life. After around two milliseconds of indecision, she decided to embrace the new version of events. She bowed and blew kisses from the stage, before grandly announcing that she would be generous enough to sign autographs for everyone in the auditorium.

She descended from the stage and bathed in the ecstatic whoops and cheers that greeted her walk. The first people to speak to her were Mr and Mrs Cussock.

"Daughter, where have you been hiding all that talent? We had no idea you had the skills required to perform in such an immersive and ground-breaking piece of theatre!" said Mr Cussock.

"Yes, we'll have you stage another show here again, this time for a full week at least. You must come back home to live with us immediately," said Mrs Cussock.

"Excuse me, Mummy and Daddy, but I have autographs to sign. If you want to speak to me about my show contract then you can join the queue," said Gloria. She barged through to the auditorium and was shortly followed by a legion of audience members who were desperate for her signature.

The New Beginning

The only people who didn't want signatures from Gloria were Miss Muddle and the orphanage children. The children didn't need signatures, because Gloria had decorated every surface of the orphanage with her handwriting, whilst Miss Muddle was too fascinated by Bethany's now dormant superstinkrats.

"So . . . this was all part of the show?" she asked. "Were the frogs in the shop a planned part of the experience as well then?"

Bethany jumped down from the stage. She saw that Miss Muddle was perfectly ready to believe anything that she had to say.

"No," said Bethany, with a sigh. "I had nothing to do with those frogs, and I was cross when you thought it was

me, so I was gonna unleash these in your shop. Super soz, Miss Muddle – I promise, I'll never come to buy sweets from you again."

Miss Muddle picked up one of the rats. "Why are you telling me?" she asked. "You could have got away without me ever knowing what you did."

"I know. But it didn't seem like a do-gooding thing to do," said Bethany. "That stuff Ebenezer said was true. I really am trying to be better – even though I'm rubbish at it."

Miss Muddle rasped a knuckle against the rat's metallic body. She shook her head with disappointment.

"You know, this is quite a clever little trick – most inventive. But you should have found a way of simulating the fur as well, otherwise it would have been way too obvious to the health inspector" she said. "When I was younger, I came up with something similar. The librarian refused to lend me a book I wanted to borrow, so I filled her sugar pot with dyed-white chilli powder."

"You were a prankster?" asked Bethany.

"Oh yes. There's a lot of overlap between pranking and sweet-making – both require a very similar set of creative skills. These days I put all my mischief into my shop," said Miss Muddle. She paused, and sized up Bethany again. "Are you still interested in working with me on the hampers?" Abso-fricking-lutely!" said Bethany.

"Good – everyone deserves another chance. Arrive at 10am on Monday in your finest apron. And I want you to have read the first *three* chapters of *Quantum Mechanics for Morons*," said Miss Muddle. "You'll be exhausted by the end of the day."

Miss Muddle turned her back before Bethany could say anything like 'Whoopee!', or 'I can't even get past the first sentence of that book!' Geoffrey quickly came running up the aisle to speak with her.

"Sorry, I couldn't help overhearing, because . . . well, because I was trying to overhear. I can't believe you're going to be a sweet-maker, that's incredible!" he said.

"Geoffrey, are you OK?" Bethany asked. She gave him a few thwacks on the arm to check that he was really back.

"Hmm? Oh, ah, yes – that puddling trick you did on me was very clever. I feel ever so refreshed," he said. "Thank you for involving me in the show, I love magic tricks!"

"Geoffrey, none of that was part of the . . ." Bethany began. But then she saw the pleased look on his face, and realised that his version of the evening might be better as it was. "Oh, never mind. You're welcome, I guess" she said, instead.

"What sweets are you going to make first?" asked Geoffrey. "The whistlepip wonders are my very favourite!"

"Then those are the ones I'll ask Miss Muddle to show me first," said Bethany. "If you like I can come and tell you about it on Monday, after I've finished."

"YES, PLEASE!" said Geoffrey. They both blushed, because he had spoken with way too much eagerness. "I mean, only if you want to, of course. We can talk about *D.I. Tortoise* as well."

"Soz. The only thing I'll be reading this weekend is *Quantum Mechanics for Morons*. I guess we'll just have to talk about something else other than comics."

"Something *other* than comics?" said Geoffrey. They both frowned as they tried to figure out what that meant. "How would that even work?"

Timothy called for Geoffrey and the rest of the children, because he wanted to get out of the building before Gloria or the Cussocks changed their mind about living together again. Geoffrey bid Bethany goodbye with a double-flappy wave, whilst she ran over to tell Ebenezer the definitely-not-a-big-deal news about her new sweet-making career. Annoyingly, Ebenezer was busy asking Mr Nickle a gazillion questions about the life of a secret agent.

"I'm flattered by your interest, Squeezer, but there's too much for me to do at present," said Mr Nickle, with a certain air of grumpiness. Frankly, he wished that there was more time in his life for charming conversations. "I need to clean up here and check whether the beast has left anything dangerous in the building. The work of D.o.R.R.i.S. must be kept orderly and hidden at all times."

"So how come you didn't wipe our memories?" asked Bethany.

"You two know more about the beast than anyone else. You can expect a call soon, as we try to learn more about the creature," said Mr Nickle. "And I let Gloria remember because no-one would believe her anyway."

The D.o.R.R.i.S. stick shook in his hand again – this time with more aggression. He looked at it in a confused and somewhat alarmed manner.

"This never happens with the other creatures," said Mr Nickle, wrinkling his wrinkly brow again.

"Are you sure Claudette's safe in there?" asked Bethany.

"Oh yes, best place in the world for her. Don't worry, I'm sure you'll be seeing her again, very soon," said Mr Nickle. He wrinkled his brow at the stick again. "All the same, I better get cracking. Goodbye, Ebenezer and Bethany."

Mr Nickle went backstage to check for any beastly remains, whilst Bethany and Ebenezer made their way back down the aisle. A wave of sadness passed over Bethany's face.

"What's up?" asked Ebenezer.

"I was just thinking about Claudette. She was so good to me, and I can't help feeling that what happened to her is our fault," said Bethany. "If it wasn't for us then she would never have met the beast. Maybe I shouldn't take Miss Muddle's job, or read comics with Geoffrey, or try and get involved in the neighbourhood – perhaps we'd be better off just keeping to ourselves."

"There's no one to blame for what happened to Claudette but the beast," said Ebenezer. "And if you really want to de-beast your life, then you must never isolate yourself from other people. It's what the beast made me do for five hundred years, and look how I turned out."

"Like a selfish gitface," said Bethany, grinning.

"Yes. Like a total selfish gitface," said Ebenezer, grinning right back at her. He had no idea that it would feel so good to have her call him that again.

They weaved their way through the crowds who were lined up in the auditorium, and went out on to the street. All the taxis outside the theatre had been taken and Claudette had crumpled the scooter, so they started the long walk back home.

"I can't believe you said I have the table manners of a warthog," said Bethany.

"I can't believe you're focusing on *that* part of the speech," said Ebenezer.

"Nah, I heard the other bits too – I even managed not to vom when you said the soppy stuff," said Bethany, grinning again. "I liked what you said about do-gooding."

Ebenezer sighed. He regretted what he was about to say, before he even said it.

"Yes. I do think you might be right about the whole do-gooding nonsense, by the way," he said in a gruff voice. "We should probably do some more of it."

"What?!" said Bethany. "This is coming from you?!"

"I didn't say I was happy about it. In fact, I had been looking forward to spending a few solid months relaxing, bubble-bathing, and drinking pots of tea," said Ebenezer. "But . . . well, the last couple of days haven't been good for do-gooding for either of us. I suppose we're obligated to try and make up for it."

"Claudette will be so proud when she hears!" beamed

Bethany. "Here's what I'm thinking we should do first . . . "

The long walk home felt even longer for Ebenezer as Bethany ran him through all the things that they would be doing over the coming days, weeks, and months. Tears of exhaustion and self-pity rolled out of his eyes as he realised that they were far from finishing their do-gooding mission. In fact, they were just at the beginning.

THE END . . . ISH

(BY WHICH I MEAN YOU
SHOULDN'T BOG OFF QUITE YET)

The Caged Beast

Three days later, Ebenezer and Bethany were standing on the most boring street in the world. It was deliberately boring – designed so that people would walk and drive past it, without ever feeling compelled to give it a second glance.

Its name was something forgettable like 'Mill Road' or 'North Street', and the buildings were constantly (and secretly) remodelled, so that changing architectural fashions would never make them anything less than 'unremarkable.'

The most interesting thing about the whole place was a puddle. Bethany splashed her sneakers in it, whilst Ebenezer rang the buzzer of the address they'd been given. A few seconds later, Mr Nickle answered through the intercom.

"*Yes, what — it?*" he asked. "*Oh hullo, Squee—er. What*

are you do— ere? How the devil did you f—nd us?"

"You invited us – remember? You woke us up in the middle of the night. You said it was important, you said we had to come here first thing," said Ebenezer.

"Yeah – and it's a total pain. Some of us still have two and a half chapters of *Quantum Mechanics for Morons* to read," shouted Bethany, from the puddle.

"*Did I really?*" said Mr Nickle, thoroughly confused. "*Why would I do th—? Are you —?*"

"Mr Nickle, We can't hear you very well. It sounds like your miles away," said Ebenezer.

"*Hmm? Oh ye– that's because I prob—ly am. Come join me. P—t on the wellies,*" said Mr Nickle.

The intercom went dead, and a few moments later, two pairs of scarlet wellington boots were pushed through the letterbox; one set in Ebenezer's size, the other in Bethany's. Ebenezer pushed the intercom again, but there was no response, whilst Bethany ran over and put her boots on.

"This'll be much better for splashing!" said Bethany.

She ran up to the puddle and jumped into it. But, instead of a great big splash, there was nothing. She disappeared inside the puddle, as if she had fallen through the earth.

"BETHANY!" shouted Ebenezer. He quickly put on

his boots and jumped after her, even though he had been feeling distinctly uncomfortable around puddles ever since the beast had done its puddling in the theatre.

He fell through the puddle as well, and discovered that it wasn't a puddle at all. It was a portal to an island.

He found himself wading in a sea of water, towards the island's shore. The island was dominated by a single building – a fat, high-tech pyramid building, covered with the letters;

D.o.R.R.i.S. HQ – Nothing to see here

Other people and creatures – agents, prisoners, interview suspects – were wading towards the shore from all directions, each of them having being transported to the island from different portals, all across the world. Bethany was already on the beach with Mr Nickle, trying her very best not to be impressed by the spectacle.

Ebenezer quickly ran up the beach towards them. Mr Nickle was leaning on one of his walking sticks and carrying three helmets under his other arm.

"Yeah, you definitely did. You said it was urgent," Bethany was saying, whilst Mr Nickle looked on in confusion.

"Was it about the beast? Or Claudette?"

"Claudette? Who's —?" began Mr Nickle, but then he remembered. He looked down at the helmets and frowned again. "I don't know why I have these, but we should put them on."

The three of them put on their helmets, as they walked into the pyramid. The ground floor lobby was a hotbed of mistrust, with agents looking suspiciously around the room – all of them silently accusing each other of treachery. Mr Nickle led them through to the medical bay, where a familiar face was snoozing upon one of the beds.

"CLAUDETTE!" said Bethany. She ran over and woke up Claudette with a squeeze.

"Oh, hullo, poppet," said Claudette. Her voice was weak and so was her body. She was hooked up to various beeping machines, and, even when she was awake, she seemed in a half-dazed state. "I'm so, so sorry about everything that —"

"Nah. Don't you dare say sorry. No one's to blame but the beast," said Bethany.

The mention of the beast caused Claudette to wince.

"That creature . . . I saw inside its mind, you know," she said. "The war, Rapscallicus, that dreadful Lady Morgana . . . there are things that these eyes will never unsee."

"Don't worry about any of that. The beast is locked away. You'll come back to the fifteen-storey house, and we can help you forget all about it," said Bethany.

"No!" said Claudette, with all the strength that she had left in her weak voice. The very suggestion of the idea seemed to repulse her. "Sorry, Bethany, but I can't come back there. Too many memories of the beast. I need to go far away. I'm going home to look after the children of Wintloria. Mr Nickle says there's a portal that leads right out onto the rainforest."

"Did I say that?" asked Mr Nickle, scratching his helmeted head. "Yes, of course I did. How did I forget that conversation?"

"I'll miss you," said Bethany, stroking the feathers on Claudette's wings.

"We'll stay in touch," said Claudette. "Don't you worry poppet, you'll never, ever get rid of me."

Claudette's eyes started to droop. Bethany gave her another squeeze, and tried to hide her sadness. Ebenezer could barely stand to watch.

"We'll both miss you, Claudette," said Ebenezer. "The children of Wintloria are lucky to have you singing them songs and laying them delicious breakfasts."

Claudette opened her eyes again, and purple tears were leaking out of her eyes. She turned her face away, as they left the medical bay.

"Did I say something wrong?" asked Ebenezer.

"Yes, it's all coming back to me now . . . " said Mr Nickle. "Claudette's been left badly damaged by the beast. She's getting stronger every day, but at the moment the only eggs she can lay are ones of boiled cabbage. And the doctors fear she may never be able to sing again."

"Poor Claudette," said Bethany. "Can't you do anything for her?"

"We're doing all we can," said Mr Nickle. "I had a long chat with the doctors about it, and yet . . . for a moment I forgot everything about her. How can that be the case?"

"Well, you are getting older," said Ebenezer.

"This has nothing to do with my age," said Mr Nickle, crossly. "It's got something to do with the mind of the beast. That's why we're wearing these helmets, I remembered something when Claudette was talking about it."

Mr Nickle walked over to the elevators. Once inside, he fiddled with the top of his stick, and revealed a panel of buttons showing floors that were only available to the head agent. Mr Nickle jabbed the button at the very top labelled 'THE CAGE'.

The elevator travelled in a diagonal slope, as they climbed to the top of the pyramid. It was a slow journey, because Mr Nickle kept stopping the elevator to look at the floors on their way up.

"Claudette wasn't the only one damaged by the battle over her body. The beast has been confused ever since we deposited it in the cage. The confusion is spreading to others, like radiation," said Mr Nickle.

The further they went up the pyramid, the more confused the people on the floors seemed to be. On one floor, a janitor was brushing his teeth with a mop. On the floor above, a dog owner had put a leash around his neck and was barking like a poodle. On the one above that, two fox-like creatures were trying to handcuff each other – both unsure about who was the agent, and who was the prisoner.

"The effects are temporary, but alarming. I fled from the beast's cage to issue these telepath helmets to everyone, but, by the time I got downstairs, I'd forgotten what I was doing," said Mr Nickle. "That must have been why I called you in, Squeezer, to help settle the beast's confused mind."

They reached the top floor of the pyramid – a single,

spacious room with a cluttering, clanking floor, and walls that were lined with trumpets. They were greeted by two smiling, dazy-eyed agents. They were carrying plasma guns, but playing them like air guitars.

"I told you to put on the helmets!" said Mr Nickle, crossly. "At least, I think I did anyway."

"Helmets, what are helmets?" asked one of the agents.

"Helmets sound delicious. We're ever so hungry!" said the other one.

Mr Nickle pushed the agents aside, and walked through to the room. Ebenezer and Bethany followed him, and saw the beast.

The beast was sat in a triple-grade laser cage, normally used to contain the spread of black holes. Its blobby back was facing them, and it was scratching its head.

"OK, I don't know what you're doing – but stop it, now," said Mr Nickle. "We'd rather keep you alive, but don't think that this will stop us from trumpeting you."

The beast turned around. It still had three black eyes, two black tongues, and a dribbling mouth, but there was something different about it. Usually, its eyes shone with fury, but now they were blank and glazed with confusion.

"Who are you?" asked the beast. Its voice was soft, but

no longer slithery. "Who's this strangely trousered man and this backpacked girl? Who am I?"

"Nah. That's not gonna work on us," said Bethany, stepping forward. "You know exactly who you are, and so do we."

"Do you, do you really? Oh, what wonderful news!" Hope flittered into the beast's three eyes. "Will you tell me who I am? Please, you're my only hope – help me."

Bethany and Ebeneezer

will return in

'THE MIND OF THE BEAST.'

Uncaged in 2022

CHECK OUT
BOOK 1

→